Protecting Paige

Book Three of The Baker Legacy Series

Beth Sorensen

For My Wonderful Neighbors
Thank you for providing friendship, support, feedback,
great parties, even better conversation,
and a cat named Paco.

Trigger Warning

Sensitive readers may find some topics in this novel disturbing. For a complete list of trigger warnings, please go to bethsoren.com and check the Content Warnings tab.

Prologue

Four Years Earlier

THE CHILL FROM THE snowy morning caused me to shiver before I looked up from my desk's phone. It was my first day working as the receptionist at The Baker's Dozen Brewing Company, and I was flying blind.

A man walked through the front door, and a blast of cold air joined him.

Noah Foster wasn't just any man, though, but rather the most gorgeous creature I had ever laid eyes on. I would later hear one of his aunts describe him as devastatingly handsome. It was the perfect description. My guess was that he ran regularly and maybe spent time in the gym. He wasn't as broad-shouldered as some of the men who worked at the brewery but was tall and muscular.

He was on the phone, laughing and being way too loud. Most of the time, I would find this irritating, but his deep voice and smart-ass attitude were anything but that.

"You fucking did what? No way. She's way out of your league. Why the hell do I think that?"

He stomped his feet on the mat at the door, removing the snow from his boots. After, he removed his gloves, hat, and coat and hung them on the coat rack placed in the lobby for guests. Then he ran his fingers through his dark brown hair, and every piece fell perfectly into place.

"Because I—" He froze when he saw me. "Dude, got to go. There's a new receptionist at the brewery."

After he ended the call, he smiled with a bright, white-toothed grin as he approached me.

When I arrived that morning, Hope Baker, the assistant production manager, gave me a ten-minute tour of the facility before handing me off to Georgia Hayes, the human resources officer. I filled out my new hire paperwork and then she sent me to an empty desk near the entrance.

It didn't take long to figure out the basics of how the phone system worked in the historic brick building, but I soon discovered the desk's extension list was outdated. It was causing a backup of lines on hold, so the last thing I needed was the distraction of a handsome man.

"Welcome to The Baker's Dozen Brewing Company. Can I help you?" I asked with a smile as Noah approached. Two steps in, he tripped on the edge of the floor mat and landed on one knee. His phone slid about five feet across the floor. And just like that, his cool, bad-boy façade melted away. Yet a still-handsome, overly awkward guy made his way to my desk after retrieving his phone.

He leaned on the counter, resting his elbows and muscular forearms. He smelled of sweet wine and vanilla.

"Uh, hi. Hi. You must be new."

Another line rang in.

"Excuse me. It's my first day," I said as I picked up the receiver. "Good morning. The Baker's Dozen Brewing Company. How may I direct your call? Henry Baker? One moment, please."

I searched the list for my new boss's extension. The list originally tucked under the phone was in no particular order.

"Fi-Fifteen," the man stuttered in a hushed tone.

As he said it, I found the name on the list. It said thirteen.

"Are you sure?" I whispered.

He nodded, and I followed his lead.

"Thank you. This list must be really old."

"Who else are people trying to reach?"

I picked up the next line on hold and asked. The man before me gave me extension numbers until all five lines were clear.

"Let me see." I handed him the paper, and he glanced at it before taking the pen from a cup on the counter. He crossed out former employees and old extensions, put new ones in, and said, "You're right. This is an ancient list. It may not be complete, but this should help."

He handed me the revised directory before offering me his hand, warm and strong. It swallowed mine, and he squeezed my hand before releasing it. When he did, his elbow hit the cup of pens on the counter. The pens scattered across the counter and desk while the cup landed on the floor. Picking up the cup, he nervously collected pens while I placed the ones I gathered into their holder.

"I'm, um, Henry's nephew. Noah, Noah Foster."

"Paige Wilson."

"Well, Paige, it's, um, nice to meet you."

"Thanks for the updated directory. Now, if I can figure out how to turn on this computer, I'll be set."

"It won't turn on?" he asked as he rounded the counter and leaned in from behind me.

When he did, his warm breath tickled the back of my neck, and I smiled.

"Ah, this is one of the new Apple computers." He gently picked up my right hand, placing it behind the lower right corner of the monitor until I felt the slightest indentation, and the warmth from his skin made mine tingle.

I pressed the button, and the screen came to life, presenting a Baker's Dozen Brewing Company logo as wallpaper.

He released my hand, and I swiveled in my chair to face him.

"Thank you. Can you do me a favor and not tell anyone I couldn't figure that out? I'm not computer-savvy, and I'd hate to lose this job before I finish my first day."

"No problem. Don't feel bad, though. This particular monitor isn't the easiest to figure out. You can't see the buttons, and nothing is labeled."

He stared into my eyes, and suddenly, the newly found smoothness in his voice evaporated with his next words, and he stared at his feet. It was strange. One minute, he was cool and confident. The next, he sounded like a nervous geek. He swung back and forth between them like a pendulum.

"Um, well, I'm here to harass my, my cousin, so I'll just go."

"Hope?"

"Yep." Our eyes locked, and he took a deep breath and slowly exhaled. "I'll, um, see ya around."

As he walked past me and up the stairs, I had a brief vision of the two of us together, and it shocked me. I didn't think about men and relationships. It was too dangerous for everyone.

Another chill ran up my spine. I wasn't sure if it was from meeting Noah Foster or the cold, blustery day seeping through the door. Either way, I would need to go thrift shopping after work in hopes of finding more sweaters appropriate for the office. Willow Creek, Virginia, was the furthest north I had ever lived, and it was only January. I would need warmer clothes to get through the winter.

Chapter One

"I T'S TIME FOR THE wedding party to join Hope and Grayson, our bride and groom, on the dance floor," the wedding coordinator said through the mic.

Within seconds, Noah was standing beside me. "Are you ready to dance?"

I nodded and took his hand. Of course I was. I had wanted to dance with Noah since the day we met four years earlier. We stepped onto the ballroom floor and began to sway to the music. Hope had a string quartet at her ceremony, but this evening's band was better suited to a reception with dancing.

I took a moment to appreciate the beautifully decorated room in his grandmother's home. Usually, the floor was covered in Turkish rugs and a long dining room table that could seat twenty-four people filled the space. That night, the furniture had been removed. White and pink flowers, along with tall candelabras and satin ribbons, decorated the room. The floors were highly polished, and candlelight reflected off of them.

It was one of dozens of changes made to the house for the reception. The Baker family lived a life of opulence I hadn't seen since I was a young child. Champagne flowed endlessly, and fresh flowers filled every table and corner of the house.

I had seen Noah dance at other events with other people and knew he could do much more, but I was glad he didn't try. I grew up in a family where dancing was not only frowned upon but downright forbidden.

As we swayed to the music, we talked.

"I know I've said it before, but you look beautiful tonight."

The man must not have known much about women's clothing. Hope had picked out the most horrible pink bridesmaid dresses known to mankind. Either that, or he liked the strapless, cleavage-baring neckline and the thigh-high slit on the skirt. Regardless, my face warmed.

"Thank you. You look great in a tux."

"All men look great in a tux. Hell, monkeys look great in a tux." He smiled at me and raised a single eyebrow. His smile lit up a room.

I had been told he was a smooth operator and had seen glimpses of it. But he was a stuttering, nervous goofball whenever we were in the same room. However, the weekend of Hope's wedding was different. He had been able to keep his nervousness to a minimum. I don't know why or how, but it was wonderful.

I had a crush on Noah Foster since the day we met but was too shy to make the first move. Even though we saw each other regularly at office lunches, holiday parties, and the annual winery celebration.

In addition, I knew the possible danger of letting someone get close to me. However, my loneliness had recently overridden my desire to keep people at a distance. Over time, I had begun to crave the social life I had enjoyed in New Orleans.

Two years earlier, I would have declined Hope's offer to be a bridesmaid, but when she asked me in November, I jumped at the chance. I was thrilled when Noah and I were paired for all the wedding activities. His enthusiasm told me he was pleased with the arrangement as well.

As we danced, our eyes locked. This was the moment little girls dreamt about. At least I had until I was ten and was taken to Ferma to live when my mother remarried. Then I dreamt of being rescued by Mr. Right from that horrible farm. It wasn't until I was nearly thirteen that I understood that the place was a cult. That's when my dreams turned to escaping from Ferma and not finding a man to live with happily ever after.

Noah was everything I could ever want. I just prayed he felt the same way. He leaned down and brushed his lips against mine. It was the perfect first kiss. When I opened my eyes, his were dark and stormy.

We continued dancing in silence before he whispered in my ear, "I want this to last more than just for tonight. I want this feeling to last forever."

"Me too."

I smiled and only broke eye contact with him to lean against him, and he tightened his arms around me.

Life had never felt so perfect.

Every time in my adult life, when I'd found contentment, my past would catch up with me, and I would have to start over again. I took a deep breath and pushed the thought away, wanting to remain focused in the moment.

We danced for a few more songs. When the music switched up a beat, we took a break. However, he took my hand when we left the dance floor and didn't let go.

It was long after midnight when I watched Faith and Ben walk away together. As soon as they were out of sight, Noah was beside me with my new lavender wool and cashmere coat in hand. Miss Vivian, both Noah and the bride's grandmother, had given one to each bridesmaid that morning. The weather was unseasonably cold in Virginia for April, and the ceremony was outside. It was the nicest article of clothing I had ever owned. She even had everyone's names embroidered on a tag inside of them to avoid confusion.

"Quick, put this on," he said as he held it for me. He already had a heavy coat on, and when I looked, others were grabbing their coats as well.

"What's going on?"

"Ben's going to propose to Faith at the gazebo. We are all going to watch."

Faith had turned him down once. However, I didn't want my night with Noah to end, so I said nothing and let his hand rest on the small of my back as he guided me out.

As we followed the group out the door, caterers followed the group with trays of glasses and champagne.

While walking, I glanced at the rows of grapevines that disappeared into darkness. "Noah, what will this frigid weather do to the grapevines? When I've been here before in the spring, the vines are much further along in their growing cycle."

He kissed the top of my head and smiled. "You are so observant. The bud break was much later this year. It will mean a later harvest, and we might lose some grapes because of it as well. The next month will tell us more about how this year's production will look. But that's a problem for another day."

When we rounded the corner of the house, thousands of tiny fairy lights came to life around the gazebo and in the large willow tree nearby. My eyes grew wide with wonderment. The tiny lights, along with the cold night air, gave the structure a magical feel. It was difficult to wrap my head around the extravagance of constructing a gazebo for this singular event.

Everyone approached the couple in the gazebo in time to see Ben on one knee. In my childhood, I had hoped for such a thing for myself. But over the last few years, I had grown to accept I would probably never marry or have children.

"I know you don't like surprises. I hope this one is okay." Ben paused nervously. "I never thought I would meet anyone as wonderful as you. It took a series of events to get us to one another that can only be accounted for by fate. It is something I will never take for granted. Ever again. So, Faith Katherine Baker, will you marry me?"

Faith stood statue still, in shock, staring at him. After a minute, Ben spoke up.

"Faith, sugar, I've had training sessions with clients that were shorter than this."

Ben was a physical therapist.

"Oh, um, okay." Ben exhaled. "We could do that someday."

He stood up and slid a massive ring on her finger before sealing the engagement with a kiss. Ben looked excited, but her answer didn't sound confident, and I wasn't surprised.

Over the last four months, Faith and I had formed a friendship over many nights of wine, pizza, and discussions about her relationship with Ben. As much as she loved him, the commitment of marriage was difficult for her. She had seen how the death of her father had destroyed her mother and feared the same fate awaited her.

Moments later, the group that formed at the foot of the steps of the gazebo to witness the event congratulated them. As I watched the scene unfold and listened to everyone tell the newly engaged couple what a fine married couple they would make, I wondered what made a good marriage.

Memories of my mom and dad would never be an example for me. I was young when my dad died, and before that, they rarely spent more than ten minutes a day in the same room. Then, when my mom remarried, her new husband was no example of how a husband—let alone a man—should behave.

Everyone returned to the main house with champagne glasses in hand as the freezing wind beat on their exposed skin.

Everyone except Noah and me. He led me into the gazebo and slowly swayed me to the faint sounds of the music coming from the house.

"Paige, I was serious about what I said earlier. I don't want these feelings I have for you to end when the sun comes up."

"I know. I meant it when I said I felt the same."

"I'm not seeing anyone else right now. I plan to keep it that way. Just you and me."

"Just you and me," I replied.

He placed a hand at the nape of my neck, holding my head in place as he delivered a long, passionate kiss. His other hand, on the small of my back, pulled me closer until we were fully pressed against one another.

As he kissed me, I wondered if this was a dream. Because if it was, I never wanted to wake up.

Chapter Two

Hours later, Noah's eyes scanned my studio apartment as we walked through the front door. Along with the other members of the wedding party, we celebrated the entire night. The sun was rising, providing a beautiful combination of gold and grapefruit-pink light throughout the room and causing beautiful reflections from the quartz crystal obelisks on the windowsills to dance against the walls.

"Very eclectic," he commented as he looked around.

However, his eyes and facial expression said more. He was shocked by how meagerly I lived. The apartment wasn't in the best part of town, so I thought he'd be prepared. As soon as he saw me staring, he changed his expression to a slightly forced smile.

He walked to the futon and took a seat. A few days after moving to Willow Creek, I found a used futon for free. It was my bed and the only piece of furniture I owned for the first three months after moving into the apartment. I wanted to replace it with a sofa but didn't want to spend the money. I was waiting until the next year when I was hopeful that my finances would be greatly improved.

"It's not much, but it's home."

Compared to Thomas Hall, it was a hovel. I was a little embarrassed but tried not to let it show.

As I slipped my shoes off, I asked Google to turn on my Sunday morning playlist, and music began softly playing from the tiny speaker on the kitchen counter. Fleetwood Mac was a favorite band of mine, and the majority of my playlists started with one of their songs. I always had music playing in my apartment. Silence was a terrifying reminder of a life long left behind.

Eclectic was a kind word for my belongings. My dining table was a white wicker patio set with a glass tabletop I found on the side of the road that I repainted. My bookcases were stacked wooden crates from the brewery. Since I couldn't paint the walls, I covered two completely in colorful jewel-tone print curtains from floor to ceiling. While it was sparse, I kept the apartment spotlessly clean and the faint scent of sage always lingered in the living room.

"I would tell you to watch television while I change, but I don't own one."

"How do you not own a television?" Noah asked as I opened the tiny closet and picked out a tunic-style sweater and jeans.

Then I fished through a basket until I found black flats. I was thankful to be out of the towering heels I had worn all night. The bridesmaid's dress I had been in for fifteen hours was tight, and it was time to change to more comfortable clothing before we met up with the rest of the wedding party for breakfast at the diner in town. Noah had changed from his tux to jeans and a sweater before we left the main house at Thomas Hall Estates and Winery, where his grandmother lived and Hope's wedding had occurred. I left the door to the bathroom cracked when I went into it so I could still hear Noah.

Once I was out of my bridesmaid's attire, I slipped the green variegated malachite talisman I wore daily over my head. When the stone came to rest on its familiar spot in my cleavage, my body relaxed. It was given to me to protect me from the evils of the world during a rushed goodbye. I was reluctant to remove the green stone, but it didn't work with the bubblegum-pink bridesmaids' dresses that clashed with everything in existence.

"Easy. I rarely watch anything but movies, and when I do, I stream them on my laptop."

The truth was that I couldn't afford both a television and a laptop. Plus, it would be more to pack should I ever need to leave quickly.

When I returned to the futon, Noah was staring at the Tarot cards on the thrift store glass-topped coffee table while scratching my cat, Paco, behind his ears. Paco, in turn, leaned against Noah and rubbed against his leg as he purred. Watching Noah give and receive affection from my beloved pet caused me to pause before sitting and smile.

"Paco likes you. They say animals are a good judge of human nature. He normally doesn't let men near him."

Paco was a twelve-year-old orange tabby I found in Nashville at the local shelter where I volunteered. I brought him home one weekend to keep me company and adopted him the following Monday. He was very much a gentleman cat whose previous owners had cruelly declawed him. He was of a sweet nature and spent much of his time basking in the sun or snuggling up to either me or visitors he liked for attention.

"You wear that necklace a lot," he said, noticing the leather cord around my neck as he continued to give Paco the attention the cat was certain he deserved. "But always tucked into your shirt. Why?"

"It's a protection stone." I pulled the necklace out. "It was a gift from a loved one a long time ago."

He frowned and looked down at the table in front of him. I was confused as to what changed his expression and hoped the tarot cards weren't the reason.

"What does all of this mean?" he asked, pointing to the tarot cards.

A complex Celtic Cross tarot card spread covered most of the small wooden coffee table.

"This tarot spread was for a friend. I should have cleaned it up after, but I was running late for the dress rehearsal." I smiled, having no intention of telling him its meaning. That was between me and his newly engaged cousin, Faith. "Have you ever had a reading before?"

"Once, at a Halloween party, when I was in high school."

"What did they say?"

"I don't think the guy they hired knew what he was doing. It was just three cards. Not all of this."

"Ah, a Past, Present, Future reading."

"That's a thing?" I nodded, and he smiled. "Cool! Wanna do mine?"

He wasn't taking it seriously, but I didn't care. I knew I would.

If asked, I would consider myself a Christo-Pagan. I believed in fundamental Christian teachings but was certain there was more. Something more ancient that tapped into nature and the deities that represented life and the universe around me.

"Are you sure? Once you know, there's no un-knowing it."

"You think you're that good?"

He definitely didn't understand. It wasn't me. It was what the universe wished to reveal through the cards. I was just a conduit. That would need to be a discussion for another day if we were to be a couple.

I stood, walked around, and lit a few candles before lighting incense in a brass holder on my coffee table. After that, I sat on the floor across the coffee table from him. When I collected the loose cards and added them to the deck, dread warned me to stop. I don't know why I didn't listen to my feelings, but I ignored them and continued anyway.

After knocking on them three times, I cleansed the cards in the scented smoke of the incense and shuffled them before Noah cut the deck three times.

"Well, now I know why you always smell like incense."

I smiled at his comment, turning the first card over and placing it on the table.

"The Fool. That's appropriate for you."

Noah frowned as he grumbled. I forgot he didn't know its meaning.

"You don't take the cards literally. The Fool represents infinite possibilities and potential. It's your 'past' card. Look at your childhood. Heck, look at your life. The world's been your oyster since the day you were born."

"True." Curious, he leaned in to get a better look.

As soon as I flipped the next card, I blushed, and his piercing brown eyes met mine. "What is it?"

"I swear I didn't plan this or stack the deck."

"Tell me."

"It's The Two of Cups. It represents things like love, intimacy, and deep feelings. Sounds like it might be time for you to meet your match. Your soulmate."

"That's my 'present' card."

"Uh, yeah."

He looked at me, and we locked eyes. We both knew what the other was thinking.

This could be it.

We could be it.

We were it.

I quickly flipped the last card upright, hoping to change the subject. I froze when I saw . . .

The Tower.

"So, this is my future. What does it mean?"

"Nothing," I snapped. "It—it means nothing." I quickly slid the cards back into the deck and dropped them into a velvet pouch.

I hoped it was fast enough for him not to remember the card. I never read The Tower to someone if I could help it. Destruction would be part of his future, but he didn't need to know that.

He stood beside me and offered me his hand in assistance from the floor.

"Seriously, what does it mean?" he asked as I stood. "I have a feeling, based on your reaction, that it's not a good card to draw."

He was right, but I wouldn't say that to him.

"It's too hard of a card to interpret on a simple three-card read."

I wrapped my arms around his neck and pulled him into a long kiss. It would distract him, and I wanted the memory of kissing him in my tiny apartment. Thoughts raced through my head, and I wondered what was about to be destroyed. Our new relationship? Something at work? Or maybe even him?

As soon as I thought of his demise, I envisioned my violent stepbrother pointing a gun at Noah. The vision felt like a punch to the gut, but I suppressed the feeling because that would never happen. At least I was pretty sure it wouldn't. I forced the thought from my head.

"We should go. We are already late," I said after we finished. "I would be willing to bet most of the wedding party is at the diner already, and I'm in the mood for their sweet potato waffles."

Chapter Three

WHEN MY ALARM WENT off Monday morning, I felt like it was going to be one of those days. I was still exhausted from the weekend, and my head pounded. I wasn't sure if it was from lack of sleep or the massive amounts of alcohol I had consumed throughout the weekend. But I got out of bed anyway.

For the second time in a month, my car wouldn't start. I already knew what was wrong with it but didn't want to spend the money. Over the previous year, the car had spent almost as much time in the shop as I had spent driving it. This left me uneasy. I hated being without reliable transportation because I never knew when I'd need to leave quickly, and lately, the lack of transportation had been more often than not.

I walked the ten blocks to work. I had to walk quicker than normal to avoid being late, which meant I wouldn't have time to stop by the bakery for breakfast. Occasionally, I treated myself to breakfast on Mondays to start the week on a positive note.

On the upside, the weather was starting to warm. Saturday, the high had only been fifty degrees. According to the weather app, it was supposed to be a beautiful spring day in the mid-sixties. While it was still a little cool for my taste, it beat the frigid weather of Hope's outdoor wedding.

I was spoiled. I spent my youth in Southern California. Even in the winter, the temperature remained around sixty degrees, and in the summer, it rarely surpassed eighty. It was the only thing I missed about California.

Regardless of the temperature, I enjoyed the view of spring flowers freshly planted in people's front yards. Most of the shop windows were decorated in pastel colors and spring designs. Willow Creek made me happy. The small town was home for me, and I never wanted to leave it. Of course, I felt the same way about the French Quarter when I lived in New Orleans as well.

As I made my way down the sidewalk toward the brewery, I had the weirdest feeling that someone was watching me. A shiver ran down my spine, and I stopped. Looking around, I saw nothing suspicious, but my mind raced. Was it possible I had been found by my family? It was always the first question I asked myself when something in my world felt off.

I was still frozen in place when a fluffy creature rubbed against my leg. It was Baxter, the Corgi who belonged to the neighbor of Ben Sutton, Faith's fiancé. Technically, Faith lived at Thomas Hall with her mom, Cassandra Baker. However, she spent more time at Ben's place than at home.

I knelt and rubbed Baxter behind the ear.

"Hey, little guy. What are you doing out in the world all alone? It's a dangerous place out here."

A voice startled me.

"She's right, Baxter."

It was Ben, holding the dog's leash. He leaned over, attached the lead, and helped me to my feet.

"Thanks for distracting him so I could catch up. Mrs. Lowenstein opened the door to sign for a delivery this morning, and Baxter decided to make a run for it. I've been helping her look for over an hour. She is so worried about him."

As he spoke, we walked together. The apartment was across the street from the brewery. And I felt safer not being alone on the street with the creepy feeling of being watched.

"I was glad to help. By the way, if I didn't say it before, congratulations on your engagement."

"Thanks. I still can't believe she said yes."

It wasn't long before we reached the intersection of the road where the apartments and the brewery sat. We hugged and said our goodbyes before heading towards our destinations.

Somehow, I still made it to work with five minutes to spare. I had yet to sit at my desk when the florist's delivery guy came through the door.

I was surprised to see him. Only a few women worked at the brewery, so his visits were few and far between.

"Hey, Max. It's been a while."

Max was a short, round guy in his late twenties with dirty blond hair and hazel eyes. When I first moved to Willow Creek, he lived in the apartment across the hall from me. Last year, he moved in with his girlfriend to a nicer apartment across town.

"It has. Looks like life is treating you well," he said with a smile.

"It is, but what makes you say that?"

"Because these are for you." He placed a vase on the counter.

The large clear vase held the most beautiful arrangement I had ever seen. Fuchsia carnations and a purple flower I didn't recognize highlighted the dozen deep pink roses and pale pink snapdragons in the variety of fresh green filler.

I stood, motionless and speechless, until Max thrust a clipboard in front of me, looking for an acknowledgment of their receipt. When I snapped out of my paralytic state, I reached for my purse to tip him, but he declined.

"No tip necessary. The sender already took care of it."

I breathed a sigh of relief, as I was pretty sure there was no money in it to tip him.

"Have a great day, Paige," Max said as he walked out the door.

I took the card from the arrangement but didn't need to read it to know who sent it.

Paige,

Beautiful flowers for a beautiful woman.

Dinner Wednesday night?

Love,

Noah

I picked up my cell and waited for him to answer. We had exchanged numbers during the activities leading up to the wedding.

"Hello, beautiful."

"Wouldn't you have felt silly if I had lent my phone to Colin or Henry?"

Both men worked at the brewery and were part of the Baker clan. Henry was the owner of The Baker's Dozen and Noah's uncle, while Colin was his Aunt Cassandra's live-in companion and one of the brewery's brewmasters.

"Probably."

"The flowers are gorgeous. Thank you."

"You're welcome. So, dinner?"

"Yes. But can we stay in town? I've got to work the next morning."

"That's fine. Anywhere you want."

"Um, I don't know."

I had trouble making decisions when given options.

"Do you like Italian?"

"Yes. I've never been to Casa de Mimmo's. Can we go there? Or is it too expensive?"

"Of course we can. I'll call and get us a table. What time?"

"I don't know. I'm usually home by five-thirty. What about you?"

"It varies. Why don't I get us a table for six thirty?"

"Okay." The office phone rang. "I've got to go. Thanks again for the flowers. See you Wednesday."

Chapter Four

Wednesday night, I paced the floor, waiting for Noah. I raced home after work to shower and change into a flower-print dress I only wore on special occasions. I wanted a new dress for the evening, but my car repairs would eat up most of my next two paychecks, so I decided against making a trip to Zoe's boutique—which was never in my budget—and settled for the dress already in my closet.

I wasn't worried that he was ten minutes late, but by thirty minutes beyond his scheduled arrival time, I began to doubt everything. Maybe he had changed his mind. He was definitely out of my league and could take his pick of any girl around.

As I sat on the sofa, giving Paco chin scratches, I wondered if Noah had chosen someone else to spend his evening with.

As these thoughts raced through my mind, my cell phone rang. I looked at the caller ID but didn't recognize the number. It had the local 804 area code, so I answered anyway.

"Hello?" I said.

There was no response. Only silence.

Paco climbed into my lap and hissed.

"Hello?"

All I could hear was heavy breathing. Something about it gave me the creeps.

"Noah, is that you? Hello?"

A sharp knock on the door caused me to jump. I ended the call and checked the peephole on the door. Noah stood outside, running his fingers through his hair and holding a bouquet of peonies in his other hand.

When I opened the door, he smiled before taking me in his arms and planting a loving kiss on my lips. My head instantly felt light, and all thoughts beyond Noah raced from my brain.

I took a moment to balance myself. "I thought the kiss came at the end of the date."

"Well," he said with a sheepish smile, "I'll be sure to give you one then as well." He stepped into my apartment and handed me the flowers.

"Thank you. They are lovely."

"Not as lovely as you," he said, causing me to blush. "Are you ready to go?"

"Let me put these in water first."

He picked up Paco and rubbed his ear. They both watched as I pulled a glass pitcher from a cabinet and filled it with water. The only vase I owned came with the flowers he had delivered on Monday, which were still at work. The pitcher came from a yard sale last fall. I hadn't needed it, but I was drawn to it, and with it being less than a dollar, I couldn't beat the price.

"Sorry, I'm late. I lost track of time in the fields with Faith. I was going to call you when I got in the car, but my phone was dead, and I didn't have a charger."

"Really? I thought everyone kept a charger in their car."

"It's a new car. I just picked it up from the dealer last night."

"You can use my car charger if you like. Lord knows I'm not using it these days."

"Why not?" he asked as he held my jacket while I slipped it on. We headed out the door, turning off the music I had been quietly playing since I had gotten home from work.

"My car won't start. From the research I did online, it looks like it needs a new alternator and a timing belt, so I'm going to have to save some money before I can repair it. I may end up needing to replace it. It's ancient, has over two hundred and fifty thousand miles on it, and is always in the shop."

"How are you getting to work?"

"Walking. It's only ten blocks, and now that Spring is here, the weather is fine for morning and evening walks."

When we reached my Toyota RAV4, I unlocked it, grabbed my pink car charger and handed it to Noah.

"I'm sure it's not your car's aesthetic, but it will do for the night."

He gave me a crooked grin and a side hug. "Thanks."

When we approached his new car, I stopped to admire it. It was a Mercedes coupe. Metallic black with a sleek design that screamed luxury. It had to have cost a fortune.

And that's when it hit me. I was going on a date with a wealthy man. He must have thought it stupid when I asked if Casa de Mimmo's was too expensive. I considered eating at the diner a splurge.

I always knew the Baker family had money. It was no secret. Usually, though, when I saw Noah, he was in jeans and a Polo shirt or his William & Mary college sweatshirt.

Glancing away from the car and over to him, it was apparent he wasn't buying his clothes at Walmart off the clearance rack or from thrift shops, like me. His pants were tailored to the perfect length, and the shoulder seam on his shirt fell precisely where it should. This realization made me feel self-conscious about my dress, and I pulled at the hem.

I found it in the Episcopal church's thrift shop, and while it was pretty, I always felt like the fit was never quite right. It was tight through the bust, a little loose in the waist, and maybe an inch shorter than I'd like it to be.

"What do you think?" he asked, pulling my attention away from clothes and back to cars.

"Very nice. Very fancy."

"Well, cars are kinda my thing." He opened the car door for me and held my hand, guiding me into the seat. Once I was buckled in, he closed the door before making his way into the driver's seat. He handed me the charger. "Could you figure out where to plug that in while I drive? I don't want us to be any later for dinner than we already are."

As Noah began driving, I looked in the obvious places and almost immediately saw it.

"Noah, hand me your phone."

He fished it from the pocket of his leather jacket and handed it to me. I placed it in the spot designed to hold a cell phone, and it began to charge.

"You don't need a cord to charge your phone in your new fancy car, Mr. Foster," I said jokingly. "It has a wireless charging pad."

"I guess I should read the manual, huh? I was tired of driving the Mustang. This was a spur-of-the-moment thing."

"Really?"

"Well, I've been thinking about getting a Mercedes for a while. And I wanted a nice car to take you out in." Before I could comment, he said, "We're here. Stay put. I'll come get the door for you."

I had never had a man hold the door for me until the previous weekend during Hope's wedding festivities. No man had ever purchased a car with me in mind, either.

As I sat waiting, my stomach filled with butterflies. I wondered what Noah thought he was going to get out of the night as he held my hand to help me out of the car.

Casa de Mimmo's was a classic Italian restaurant. The square tables were covered in red checkered tablecloths, where the centerpiece of each table was a chianti bottle with a wax-dripping candle producing a soft glow. Oil paintings covered the walls, and Italian opera music played in the background.

After we were seated, Noah ordered a bottle of wine before we opened our menus.

"What's good here?" I asked, overwhelmed with the number of options.

"Everything."

I continued to stare at the menu, chewing my bottom lip.

Noah must have looked up from his menu at some point because, moments later, his hand was holding mine.

"Don't stress," he said. "It's only dinner."

"I'm not good at making decisions sometimes. I was never allowed to choose anything growing up, and I get anxious when there are too many choices."

Shock and confusion flew across Noah's face. Only then did I realize I had disclosed a piece of information about myself that alluded to my bizarre childhood.

He quickly composed himself and gave my hand a small squeeze before releasing it.

"Then, let me order for you." He took the menu from me and closed it. "Do you like seafood?"

"Yes, I love seafood."

"Any food allergies?"

"Not that I know of."

I was still answering his last question when the waitress returned, and Noah pointed to several places on the menu. The waitress smiled and walked away.

"See? Easy." I smiled, and he continued. "I don't want you to ever feel stressed when I'm around. We took a moment to enjoy our glasses of chianti before Noah started asking questions."

"Where did you grow up?" Noah asked.

He had no idea this very question would cause the anxiety he had just tried to quell.

"Southern California."

I had spent years crafting the story I was about to tell. While most of it was true, it was carefully curated to project a normal childhood.

"Where?"

"I lived in Beverly Hills until I was ten and then on my stepfather's farm until I left home."

In reality, the farm was a cult encampment I ran away from right after my sixteenth birthday. But he didn't need to know that—not yet.

"How did you end up in Virginia?"

"I had friends who moved to DC and invited me for a visit. We ended up at the Winter Carnival in Willow Creek. I fell in love with the place and moved here."

A long silence exaggerated my shallow breaths from nervousness. His expression told me he wasn't buying my story. No one had ever questioned it before.

I bit my lower lip.

"That sounded a little too rehearsed."

"My childhood or how I ended up here in Willow Creek?" I asked.

"Both. Why do I have a feeling that's not the whole story?"

I looked up from the silverware I had been staring at, worried that if I looked into his eyes, he would know how right he was.

"It's not, but it's all you want to know, trust me."

He was about to argue the point when our food, thankfully, arrived. Noah had the chicken marsala. He ordered me a fantastic dish I would later learn was cannelloni di mare. Homemade tube-shaped pasta stuffed with shrimp, crab, scallops and cheese with a tomato and lobster cream sauce. It was delicious and a large enough portion to provide me with dinner the next night as well.

As we ate, I changed the subject by asking him questions about his friends and family, career, and hobbies. Some of the things I knew, but others were intriguing bits about his life I had never heard.

We were nearly done eating when Noah dropped his fork and frowned.

"What's wrong?"

"You're wearing that necklace again?"

"Okay?" I didn't understand how a simple piece of jewelry could cause Noah such dismay. "So, what's the problem?"

"Well, we're on a date, and you are wearing jewelry that another man gave you."

"I never said it was from a man. Where did you get that from? It wasn't given to me by a man."

"Oh." He relaxed, and I clasped the carved malachite stone as I spoke.

"Noah, this was given to me by a woman I consider my second mother. It's a protection talisman."

"Oh, God, Paige. I'm sorry. I get jealous so easily. I just assumed that when you said a loved one, you meant a guy you loved once."

It was obvious he was upset with himself.

"Why do you think you get jealous?"

"I don't know," he sighed, looking pensive. "I've been burned in a lot of my past relationships. Maybe that's why."

"Fair enough. If it eases your mind, I haven't been on a date since I moved to Willow Creek. I know you can't say the same, and that's okay."

"Thanks."

His cheeks turned a soft shade of pink for a moment before he picked up his fork and continued eating.

Once we were both stuffed with our meals and my leftovers were packed up and bagged, we decided to go for a walk in the park before heading back to my place. It was a beautiful night with a clear, star-filled sky and a waning crescent moon.

As we strolled down the path along the creek, I knew it was time for me to give him the talk.

"Noah, how are you expecting this date to end?"

"Expecting or, uh, hoping? Because that's—that's two different answers."

"Expecting."

"A hug and a kiss when we say goodnight at your door."

I smiled. "Hoping?"

"To, well, um, well, to wake up next to you in the morning."

I think he was thankful for the dim streetlights, which hid his expression. It was the first time I had heard nervous, stuttering answers from him in over a week.

"It might be a while before we get there," I whispered. "There are things about me you don't know."

He stopped walking and quietly laughed. "You'll tell me when you're ready. Until then, well, we—we can take things one step at a time. Um, okay?"

"What's so funny?" I stopped and turned to face him.

Noah faced me as well and rested one hand on my cheek.

"It's what you do to me. Before we met, I was a cool guy. Never intimidated by anything or anyone."

"Is that so?"

"But when we are together, I don't know. I just don't want to fuck this up. I've wanted to take you out for a long time. I don't want to screw things up by saying the wrong thing."

I smiled, nodded, and breathed a sigh of relief.

"Trust me. I feel the same way." I stood on my toes and brushed my lips against his.

When I was done, the hand on my cheek was at the nape of my neck, and I repeated the gesture more firmly.

As much as I wanted to lose myself in the moment, not knowing how to tell him what he needed to know about my past, it left my mind racing. When the kiss was over, his hand slid out of my hair, and his strong arm wrapped around my waist and pulled me close as we began to walk again.

The following morning, I stepped out of my apartment to find a clear blue sky and a black Mercedes idling in the parking lot. The car pulled up to meet me at the curb in front of the apartment building's door.

I smiled when the passenger's side window rolled down and Noah leaned over and said, "Good morning. Your chariot awaits."

Seconds later, Noah was out of the car and holding the passenger's side door open for me. I gave him a quick kiss on the cheek and smiled as I got into the car. There, I found an iced oatmilk chai latte and a bag containing a cheese Danish waiting for me.

I buckled in, and when Noah was back in the driver's seat, I leaned over and kissed his cheek again.

"How did you know these are some of my favorites?"

"I've known you for a few years, and I've paid attention. You never order coffee, usually tea and occasionally cocoa, but only when it's freezing outside. And you love anything with cheese."

He wasn't wrong, but I was shocked and touched he had been so observant.

"So, what brings you into town this morning?"

"Just taking you to work."

"You mean to tell me you drove from Thomas Hall just to drive me ten blocks before driving back? That's going to eat up nearly an hour of your morning."

"And get you breakfast from the coffee shop."

My eyes filled with tears. His overwhelming care and devotion so soon into our relationship touched me deeply.

"Noah?"

He pulled into a parking spot at the brewery next to the door before looking at me. When he saw my overwhelmed expression, he leaned over the console and wrapped me in a hug.

"Babe, it's okay. You're not used to being treated like this, are you?" I shook my head, and he sighed. "You deserve so much more than you've had. You should be treated like a queen. So, as long as you'll let me, that's what I'm going to do."

"Okay," I whispered, letting him hold me a few more minutes. "I should probably go in. It's almost time for me to start my day, and you have to get back to the winery."

He put his hand under my chin and gently guided my lips to his. After we were done, I thanked him, collected my things, including my breakfast, and headed into the office after watching Noah drive away.

I sat at my desk and organized things for the day when my phone buzzed with a text from Faith.

Am I understanding that my cousin drove into town this morning just to drive you to work?

And he brought me breakfast.

Next thing you know he'll be sending you flowers.

He did that Monday.

And brought me flowers when he picked me up for our date.

Really? All of that and dinner last night? He's trying hard to make an impression.

He didn't have to try. I've been impressed for years.

Question though: why now?

I guess my goofball cousin finally got his act together.

Chapter Five

AROUND TEN O'CLOCK FRIDAY morning, my phone buzzed. It was a text from Noah.

> Coming into town for a PT appointment in an hour. Want to have lunch after?

> Sure. Are you okay?

> Yeah. Ben's helping me with my shoulder. I've been having issues with it again.

> Okay. Come get me when you're ready.

Noah was an avid basketball player. He played organized ball from the time he was seven until he graduated from college. He was a great player but knew he wasn't anywhere near NBA-level, especially since he had battled rotator cuff injuries since high school.

As an adult, he had court-side season passes for the Washington Wizards and played nearly every weekend either on the court at Thomas Hall or at the rec center with his childhood friends.

We ended up at the diner, which was a favorite place for both of us. However, the moment we walked in, I had an uneasy feeling we were being watched.

Once we ordered, the waitress brought our drinks.

Noah furrowed his eyebrows. "Is something wrong? You've looked tense ever since we got here."

"Did you ever get the feeling you were being watched? I don't know, but ever since we sat down, I feel like I'm being watched."

He smiled, first patting my hand and then holding it.

"It's not you. It's me. The Bakers get watched everywhere we go here in town. You'll get used to it."

I wasn't convinced the creepy feelings that haunted me were because of Noah's family's prominence in the community. However, I didn't want our entire lunch to focus on it, so I changed the subject.

"How was your session with Ben?"

"Good. It was just the first session. I know it won't fix all my shoulder issues, but it will definitely help."

"I'm glad to hear it. I can't be dating a guy who's falling apart."

He smiled broader, leaned across the table, and brushed his lips against mine. "Yeah, we can't let that happen."

He had just finished his words when the waitress arrived with our meals. Noah had a Rueben, and I had a grilled cheese with bacon and a cup of tomato soup. While the food was delicious, being with Noah was even better.

We lingered as long as we could, but all too soon, it was time for me to get back to work.

Noah gently guided me to the front of the restaurant with his hand on the small of my back.

"Let me get the door for you, babe," he said as he reached for the handle.

I met his eyes. "You really are so sweet."

I was about to continue when I slammed into a human wall blocking the entrance. I looked up at the person before I sucked in a deep breath.

"Oh, shit."

My world shifted on a dime, and my life in Willow Creek as I knew it was over.

It was my stepbrother, Vlad. It had been over a decade since we had been face-to-face. He looked like a cross between a Russian mobster and an Amish farmer. He was tall, with buzz-cut short blond hair and biceps the size of tree trunks. However, his weathered face now showed his age, with wrinkles around his eyes and across his forehead.

It took a minute for reality to set in, and when it did, my world tilted as though I had been sucked into a tornado. All the years of running had been for nothing. I had foolishly believed the Orlov family would eventually give up and leave me alone. I was naive to think so and terror raced through my body, leaving the bitter taste of adrenaline in my mouth.

Vlad reached out to grab my arm, so I stepped back, lost my balance on the threshold, and landed in Noah's arms.

He wrapped them around me and turned, so I was behind him, using his body to create a barrier between Vlad and me.

"If you're smart, you'll get out of the way," Vlad said.

Noah moved closer to him until they were toe to toe.

The sound of Vlad's voice brought back haunting memories.

"Not happening. Who the fuck are you anyway?" Noah's voice was deep, commanding, and loud.

"Her fiancé."

Those words coming from Vlad's mouth made me nauseous.

Before anyone else could speak, a voice called out from behind Vlad.

"Excuse me, but I can't stand here all day. You need to move, sir."

It was Mrs. Lowenstein. She was flustered, and her lips were pinched tightly together.

I watched the bluish vein pop on Vlad's forehead. It always did when he thought a woman was being disrespectful or disobedient to him.

However, when Mrs. Lowenstein put her hands on her hips and tapped her foot on the ground, Vlad stepped outside and let her through.

As soon as she made her way in, Noah stepped outside as well.

I tried to follow him, but Mrs. Lowenstein stopped me. "Paige, how lovely to see you. You looked so beautiful at the wedding—"

"Thank you. I'm sorry, I can't talk right now. I'm late returning to work from lunch. It was nice to see you again. Let's catch up soon."

The statement was true, but that wasn't why I was in a hurry. I was worried about what was going on outside, so I stepped onto the sidewalk, only to hear Vlad repeating himself to Noah with his light Russian accent.

"She's my fiancée. She belongs to me."

"No, you're not. You are nothing to me."

My body shook in fear, and my stomach roiled, but I knew Noah would do whatever it took to keep me safe. He started by, once again, creating a human barrier between me and Vlad.

"Pet, we're leaving. It's time to go home. Our father is expecting us tonight. It's time to go home to California."

Noah growled when Vlad called me Pet, but Vlad had always used that nickname from the day I arrived at the farm until I left. As a child, I often wondered if he meant it as an abbreviation of my name or if he thought of me as a house pet, like a puppy or kitten.

I wrapped my arms around Noah's waist, pressing my chest to his back, and held him tight. "Don't call me that, Vlad. My home is here. In Willow Creek. And that man is your father, not mine."

"You are marrying me next month. And when we get home, you will pay for this behavior. You want to act like a little slut? Fine, I'll tie you up and let every man at home have you. You will wish you never left Ferma."

I had forgotten after so many years how menacing and deep his voice sounded. And I knew from experience his threats weren't idle ones either.

"I don't think so. Even if you weren't my stepbrother, I would never marry you, you asshole. Not after all of the vile, disgusting, unholy things you did to me." Bile rose in my throat. "For God's sake, I was only a child."

That was the way it was done in my stepfather's family. You married a stepsibling if you had one or a cousin. Maybe even an aunt or uncle. Siblings had even been matched together. The whole idea of consummating a marriage with a blood relative grossed me out. Even at twelve, I knew it was wrong. However, as a woman, if you refused, you would suffer physical violence from at least one member of the family. And on occasion, that violence ended in death.

"Your stepbrother? What the fuck?" Noah asked but didn't pause for an answer. "Paige, get in the damn car. I'll deal with this asshole."

"You think you can handle me, pretty boy?"

"Yeah, I know I can," Noah said, his voice deep and commanding.

"Her name is not Paige. It's Petya. Petya Orlov. And I ought to know. I've been hunting her for over ten years."

It was the first time I had been called that since I left Ferma, and my stomach churned. With every word Vlad spoke, I relived the terror he had instilled in me.

"I don't know who the fuck you think you are, but this woman's name is Paige, not Petya."

Noah had relocated us, so we were in front of his car, which was luckily parked in front of the diner.

He turned to me, continuing to block Vlad from me. As he did, he whispered into my ear with a gentle voice that he only used with me as he handed me his keys, "Get in my car and lock the doors."

Before I could move, I heard a familiar voice.

"Is there a problem here?"

It was Brian Hayes. Chief of Police for Willow Creek. He was in full uniform, having just come from court.

I wanted to speak, but words would not form. Luckily, Chief Hayes had known Noah since he was a child.

"Brian, this asshole is trying to kidnap Paige and take her to California with him. Against her will."

"Is that true, Paige?"

I nodded, feeling queasier than ever.

Chief Hayes turned to Vlad. "Sir, I'm going to need some ID."

"He won't have any," I whispered as I struggled to inhale. "The Orlov cult doesn't believe in government identification. His name is Vladimir Orlov."

My body slumped into Noah's arms. He easily held me up as my breathing continued to labor.

"Paige, are you okay?" the chief asked.

My lunch was working its way back up when I turned and pushed Noah and the chief out of my way. The seemingly endless stream of vomit covered Vlad's leather jacket and jeans.

"Cyka *bitch*, I swear you will pay for this, all of this! Do you understand?!"

His anger caused him to slip the Russian word into his speech.

Red-faced, he lunged in my direction as he pulled his fist back, but Noah planted a right hook to his cheekbone and nose before he could reach me.

I had never seen Noah this angry or this violent. And while I felt safe with him, his behavior was jarring.

He got a second punch off before Chief Hayes grabbed Vlad and said, "That's enough, Noah."

He was preparing for another hit, but grabbed Vlad by the collar instead. "Touch her and the police will be dragging your dead body out of a fucking dumpster, not away from my fist, asshole."

"You need to get out of here, now, or I'm going to have to lock you up, too," the chief said more forcefully than before.

Noah ignored him, taking a moment to roll his shoulder before handing me a neatly folded cotton handkerchief from his back pocket.

"Babe, you done? Or is there more coming?"

His tone was so different from what he had used seconds earlier. It was as if someone had flipped a switch inside of him. It was soft and caring.

"I think I'm done."

Brian turned to him. "Go. I've got questions for this guy."

Vlad planted his feet. "I do not acknowledge your authority."

This was the standard line all members of the Orlov clan were taught to say if ever confronted by any law enforcement agency.

The chief ignored him.

"I'll call you later. Keep Paige close until then." He yanked Vlad's arm as he dragged him down the street to his cruiser.

The idiot fought the police chief all the way to the car, spouting obscenities in Russian at a thoroughly unimpressed Chief Hayes.

Noah loaded me into the passenger's seat, buckled me in, handed me a bottle of water previously tucked into the pocket on the back of the seat, and closed the door. He rounded the front of the car, and before he sat behind the wheel, he was on the phone.

"Gran, Paige and I have a problem."

Noah had called his ninety-year-old grandmother, Vivian Baker. It didn't surprise me that he called her.

As matriarch of the family, she was also the fixer. Whenever something went amiss with any member of the Baker family, Miss Vivian was the person who could—and would—get things back on track.

They spoke for only three minutes. It was just enough time for him to give her an overview of the last ten minutes, which included the arrival of my stepbrother, my real name as an Orlov, and Brian Hayes's presence. They weren't on speaker, so I didn't hear her reaction.

When he got off the phone, I turned to him. "I'm sorry. I guess I have some explaining to do."

"Don't apologize. Something tells me that I should have let you tell me more the other night, though."

"We should go someplace and talk," I said calmly, as though a different person was speaking and not the girl who had just seen her abuser for the first time in a dozen years. "I'll call Henry and ask for the afternoon off. If he needs me at the brewery, we can talk after work."

"No calls. We are going to Thomas Hall. I'll talk to my uncle and fix the rest later."

He took the long way around to Thomas Hall, but we didn't talk. He glanced at me while driving and occasionally used one hand to massage his shoulder. I kept my eyes on the road while sitting in the passenger's seat with my hands clasped. It probably showed on my face, but my mind raced with what to do next. The only viable option was to leave. And while it was the right thing to do, the smart thing to do, it broke my heart just thinking about it.

If I stayed, I would put Noah and his family in danger, and I would have no part in that. I recently watched Faith's fiancé, Ben, do exactly that and knew it wasn't a smart solution. I was one of only a few people who knew of Ben's role in the events over the last five months. Faith nearly being hit by a car, the brewery's roof being destroyed, and Faith's kidnapping. She told me everything during one of our evenings together over a bottle of wine. She didn't want the family to know about it all and needed a friend to talk to. Her secret was safe with me.

Instinctively, I made a list of everything I needed to do before leaving town. Collect important papers, email my resignation to Hope and Henry, pack only essentials, and make Paco as comfortable as possible while traveling. I could do all of that in a couple of hours, which meant I could be on the road before sunrise. But I would need to rent a car, as repairing mine would take too long. I'd have to abandon the RAV4 in the parking lot of my apartment complex.

As for the remainder of my belongings, I'd get Faith or Nicole, another bridesmaid from Hope's wedding I'd become friends with, to box everything up and donate them because I wouldn't be coming back.

Noah pulled into the circular driveway in front of the main house, but when I went to open the passenger door, he grabbed my hand.

"I won't let you leave Willow Creek. I know that's what you were planning on the ride here, but I will not let that happen. We will go in and talk to Gran, but I already know what we are going to do next. You are going to move in with me, and I'm going to talk to Uncle Henry about you and Violet switching positions. She can work the front desk at the brewery, and you can take her place at the winery. Thomas Hall is more like a compound than an estate. We can keep you safe here."

While Thomas Hall was an estate and winery, over the last twenty-five years, the security of the grounds had transformed from open fields and invisible property lines to twelve-foot-tall barbed wire fences and a gatehouse with an entire security team available to the Baker family twenty-four hours a day, seven days a week.

Everything I had been thinking must have shown on my face. I wanted to scream at him for being so bossy but said nothing. Instead, I sucked in air through my teeth, rolled my eyes, and frowned at him before turning my head toward the car door window.

He sounded exactly like my stepfather when he decided something for me.

Noah could tell he had overstepped my boundaries. He hurried out of the car, walked around, and opened the door for me.

Once on my feet, I found myself encased in his arms.

"I'm sorry," he whispered before kissing the top of my head. "I didn't mean to sound so dictatorial. It's just that I feel like I finally have you where I want you in my life, and I don't want to lose you. I don't think I could live with myself if I let anything happen to you."

Any frustration I was holding onto evaporated. He was trying to be caring, not controlling. I was going to have to learn the difference. I was going to have to let myself trust him.

Unconditionally.

Chapter Six

BEING AT THOMAS HALL was like stepping onto a movie set. It never seemed real. Over the years, I had read a great many books and watched dozens of movies with Southern plantation homes as their settings. Thomas Hall could have been the location of any one of these fictional mansions.

The original main house, one of many homes on the estate, was burnt to the ground during the Civil War and rebuilt on the same foundation once the war ended. Its tall white columns and multiple chimneys punctuated its antebellum style.

We were met at the door by a member of the staff and were asked to follow him. When we reached the library, we found Miss Vivian, whom the family called Gran. She was waiting, along with Noah's Aunt Cassandra, Uncle Henry, his mother, Phoebe, and a variety of finger foods and sweets in addition to tea. I was amazed at how quickly everyone arrived and how fast the kitchen pulled everything together.

Everyone made their way to us before we could reach the sofa. Henry approached me first, pulling me into a bear hug before putting me at arm's length to assess my well-being. He gave great hugs.

Phoebe was doing the same to her son.

"Look at me," Henry said, and I turned my attention from Phoebe and Noah to him. "Are you okay?"

All the voices in the room ceased.

"I think so. Yes. Maybe. Thank God Noah was with me. I think Vlad would have snatched me up and put me in a car if he hadn't been there."

Before I could say more, Phoebe wrapped an arm around me and guided me to the sofa. "What can I do to help? Are you thirsty? Hungry?"

"I still feel a little queasy. Maybe some tea would settle my stomach."

My hands were shaking, and I wondered how I would manage a teacup without spilling.

"I'll fix it," Cassandra said, in her always calm, soft voice.

"Noah needs an ice pack for his shoulder," I said.

One of the staff slipped out and returned moments later with one for him.

Once most of us were seated, Noah opened his mouth to speak, but Gran beat him to it.

"Paige . . . You *do* prefer Paige to Petya, don't you?"

"Yes, ma'am."

"I doubt you're aware of this, but the family hired a detective to investigate you when you started spending time with Faith and Hope socially," Vivian began. I shook my head. "You did a good job of covering your tracks. No one could find anything about you before you lived in New Orleans except that you bought a car in Las Vegas. We had no idea until Noah called me that you were once Petya Orlov."

"I hated to leave New Orleans. I was happy there."

As I spoke, Cassandra handed me a hot cup of ginger peach tea. It was delicious.

"Do you know what's happened since you left New Orleans? Have you stayed in contact with anyone?"

"No. When I left, Miss Genevieve, the woman who took me in, told me not to look back. She said she didn't want to know where I was either. She said the fewer people that knew, the safer I would be."

Miss Vivian frowned as she stood. She walked over to a desk and stared at it as if she were internally debating something. Then she retrieved a file folder from the top drawer and handed it to me.

"That is a file of what little the detective was able to find out about you. However, before you open it, I should warn you what's in there isn't pretty. You need to brace yourself, my dear."

My heart sank as I stared at the folder in my lap, but couldn't bring myself to open it. Nothing but death and despair radiated from it, and I felt a pull to run from this information. Finally, Noah, who sat beside me, grabbed it and opened it.

The angle at which he held it prevented me from reading it. I watched his eyes go wide as he quickly read and flipped through the pages.

"Where did you go after you left New Orleans?" he asked.

"Nashville."

"And after that?"

"DC. I stayed with a couple who were friends of mine. They died in an apartment fire about three months after I moved here."

As we spoke, I watched Noah's eyes dilate and the tension in his jaw set.

I reached out to take the file from him, but he held it away from me, just out of my grasp.

"Babe, you don't want to read this. You don't need to know."

"No. I need to see it. Not knowing won't change its contents. And I have a feeling it's important."

He was trying to protect me, but I took it and read it anyway. The only thing about me was the purchase of the car but the file contained three newspaper articles, the most recent on the top. I only read the headlines, and I read them out loud.

"'*Six Dead in Georgetown Apartment Fire.*' That's the fire that Annette and Rob died in."

I turned the page.

"'*College Roommates Killed in Home Invasion.*'"

I knew the house. I knew these people. They were my roommates in Nashville.

It was the last article that destroyed me. I hadn't finished reading the headline before tears filled my eyes, and my voice cracked.

"'Beloved French Quarter Shop Owner Shot and Killed During Robbery.'"

I stared at the article until I saw Miss Genevieve's name. The woman who loved me, took me in, and cared for me was gone. She had saved my life in so many ways, and I was to blame for her death. I pushed down the growing rage, knowing who had killed her. Clenching my teeth, I inhaled deeply. Once I calmed myself, I looked at Henry.

"Everyone I lived with after leaving Ferma is dead. There's no doubt my stepfather is responsible for this. But you let me work at the brewery anyway? Are you crazy?"

"Ferma?" Phoebe asked.

"It's the name of the Orlov Cult compound. It literally means 'The Farm' in Russian."

Henry didn't wait for either of us to say anything.

"We knew you were running from something. But you were sweet, kind, and a great employee. There was no reason for you not to stay."

"How did you know I didn't do this? For all you know, I could be a serial killer."

"I think I'm a better judge of character than that," Henry said, smiling.

I barely nodded once before Miss Vivian spoke up.

"While we were waiting for you to arrive, we've decided what we think you should do. I want you to move here. I have plenty of rooms, and we can keep you safe. We keep good security on staff twenty-four seven."

"Cassandra and Henry think you and Violet Hamstead should switch jobs for a while. The brewery is too easily accessible to the public. Violet will enjoy being able to walk to work. She might never want to trade back."

Noah smiled. "I told her as we arrived that's what was going to happen—except for one detail: She's moving in with me."

"No," I said.

The tears I didn't want to shed were trying to fall, as I was determined not to cry. However, a few managed to escape, and it irritated me that I could not control my emotions.

"What?" they all asked.

I brushed the tears away. "I can't let you do this. I won't put any of you in danger, and that's what I'd be doing if I stayed. It would be better for everyone if I just . . . disappeared."

My voice cracked as I pushed the words out.

"You are safer with us than you are alone. I appreciate your concerns, but you're part of the Baker family, and we take care of our own," Henry said.

Miss Vivian looked at me momentarily and then made her way to me, resting her hand on my shoulder. "We are going to get through this. We will not let anything happen to you."

That's when I buried my head into Noah's arm and sobbed.

Never had I experienced this level of love and the thought of running from it was heartbreaking. As I cried, Noah held me and gently rubbed my back. He would be the person I missed the most. However, the newspaper articles confirmed something I had long denied. I was being hunted by the Orlov cult. And they would never stop until they bagged their prey.

Once I regained control of myself, I sat up, and Vivian passed me a tissue from the box on the table beside her.

I blotted my face and sipped some tea. "I don't think any of you understand."

They didn't understand and could probably sense my frustration levels rising.

"My stepdad is determined to marry me back into the family. He won't stop until I'm married. I'm not going to let that happen, but I can't stay here."

"Why is he so determined?" Cassandra asked.

"A couple of reasons. First but probably the least important, in his opinion, is that I'd expand the gene pool. There's a lot of incest within the Orlov cult, and it's starting to show in the newest generation of kids. My stepfather rules over the family cult. He's the patriarch for all three hundred and twelve members. At least that's how many there were when I left and every last one is related to the others."

"So, most of the members of the cult are blood-related?" Phoebe asked.

Her voice was laced with disgust.

"All. All but me and Mom. Looking back, we were only brought in for the money and baby-making."

The thought made me ill and looking around, their expressions confirmed I wasn't the only one who found it all reprehensible.

"The second reason is money. That one seemed more important to my stepfather because the day I left Ferma, I grabbed a file folder with my name on it of important papers. In it, I discovered I have a trust fund that matures when I turn thirty. It was only then that I understood why I was so important to my stepdad. It takes a lot of money to keep Ferma running, and marrying me into the family would probably be enough to let him run it for a long, long time. Women at Ferma aren't allowed to have money. It keeps them from leaving."

"Trust fund?" Henry asked.

"My father, my biological father, was one of the Hollywood Wilsons."

Miss Vivian smiled. "You were the famous movie director, Oscar Wilson's child. I remember seeing pictures of you as a newborn in *People* magazine."

"Yes, ma'am."

"So, how do we keep this psycho stepbrother from kidnapping and marrying you?" Henry asked firmly, making sure we stayed on topic.

"You marry me instead," Noah said without hesitation. "He can't marry you if you're already married. Then he'd have no reason to try to take you from here."

I froze in place, not certain I heard him right.

Proposing marriage was the last thing I expected to hear from him that day.

"Don't be ridiculous. You barely know me."

"Then, we'll have a lifetime to get to know each other."

"Noah?" My voice dropped to a whisper, and I shook my head. "This is crazy."

"Do you think it could work to get the Orlovs off your back?" Phoebe asked.

I thought for a moment. "I don't know. If he's crazy enough to kill people who helped me, he might be crazy enough to kill anyone who marries me."

"I'm not opposed to the idea of a marriage, but maybe we need to consider a backup plan," Phoebe said, no doubt wanting to keep her son safe.

"I still think getting married is for the best." Noah leaned over and whispered in my ear, eagerly. "It's a win for me no matter what. I would finally be able to call you mine."

"You don't have to marry me to do that."

Noah cupped my face in his hand, gently rubbing his thumb against my cheek. He leaned down and placed his forehead on mine while staring into my eyes. Everything and everyone around us disappeared.

At that moment, it was just the two of us.

"Please, marry me," he whispered, love dripping from his voice.

While Noah was thinking with his heart, my decisions were coming from a place of fear. If I pushed the fear aside and listened to my heart, it matched his.

Marrying him would be the easy thing to do, but what would it cost us? Vlad was like his father. Relentless. I needed to leave for everybody's safety.

Silence draped the room while everyone waited for my response. But I didn't answer his question.

"Well?" Cassandra asked, snapping the two of us back to where we were and who we were sitting with in the library.

Blushing at our total disregard for everyone else, I said, "I don't know. I need to think about it. But I'll stay at Thomas Hall. At least for now."

That's what I wanted everyone to believe. Their lives depended on that hope. But as I said the words, I felt the restriction of being confined to Thomas Hall. As much as I loved the place, I didn't like the idea of being forced to stay there. Not fleeing was a bad idea, but between the Baker family's determination and my feelings for Noah, it would be hard to convince myself to go.

Chapter Seven

T HAT NIGHT, I STOOD in the silent house Noah and I would live in, holding Paco. I scratched under his chin while staring at two moving boxes and trying not to let the lack of sound unnerve me.

Vivian had sent a crew of people over to pack up my apartment and bring my belongings to Thomas Hall. When they arrived, the door was busted open, and the place was destroyed. Only Vlad would do something like that. My guess was that he waited for me to leave for work that morning before breaking in and ruining everything.

After the police report was filed, the crew went through every item in the apartment and placed the salvageable items in boxes—two small boxes. While the police would never find enough proof to make an arrest, even Chief Hayes knew who was responsible for the destruction.

But my belongings weren't my greatest concern. When the moving crew arrived at my place, Paco was nowhere to be seen.

Around five-thirty, I received a call on my cell. I had a prepaid phone. Having a full cellphone account would be too easy to trace.

The call was from the neighbors who lived below me. John and Jake were a lovely couple who had me down for dinner at least once a month. They arrived home from work to discover that Paco had pushed the kitchen window screen in and was napping on their bed. He had done this several times before.

It was the only thing he did on the rare occasion he ventured from the apartment on his own. When they brought Paco upstairs, with the intention of returning him to me, they found police tape covering the door and phoned me. I was so overwhelmed with relief I couldn't speak from sobbing.

Noah took the phone from me, talked to my neighbors, and made arrangements to reunite me with my beloved cat.

Vivian immediately sent a car to get him and a second employee to the pet store for supplies. I was amazed that Vivian cared so much for me that retrieving my cat was a priority to her. Paco is the only cat I have ever known that moved from one home to another via limo.

Noah had been living at the pool house, but his mother insisted we take her house, and she would move into the main house with her mother.

I would soon discover that Noah's mom, Phoebe, had planned on moving in with Vivian within the next few months anyway. The family had recently grown concerned about her and wanted someone in the family to be in the house. Especially at night, after most of the staff was gone.

The pace at which things happened that afternoon was mind-boggling. In under six hours, my apartment had been cleared out, with the salvaged items boxed and brought to me. Phoebe had collected her belongings and the few pieces of furniture she wanted, moving them to the main house. And Noah's things were brought over from the pool house.

I was still staring at the boxes when Noah walked up behind me, wrapped his arms around my waist, and gently pulled me against him.

"What can I do for you? You are so tense."

"Can you put some music on please? Silence is hard for me. I need noise."

"Okay," he said, releasing me and pulling out his phone. "What would you like? Pop, jazz, sixties music?"

"It doesn't matter. Anything."

Within seconds, jazz softly played through the speakers in the house, and Noah had me wrapped in his arms from behind once again.

"So, two boxes and Paco is all that's left of your entire apartment?"

"Yep, it's all gone. Books, clothes, furniture. It's all been destroyed."

"I'm sorry, babe. We'll get you whatever you need next week. Why the clothes, though?"

"The Orlov family would have considered them slutty and sinful. You could see skin."

"I like seeing your skin," he said, brushing the back of his hand along my arm, causing me to shiver, and I giggled. "What about your tarot cards?"

"All of my spiritual things were destroyed, too. My tarot cards were ripped to shreds, my incense box smashed, and all of the candles were broken. It's all gone."

"We'll start replacing things for you next week. Okay?"

I nodded.

"The only thing that I'm surprised Vlad let survive is a small photo album. I think he missed it. There are pictures and postcards I've collected over time in it."

I leaned back into him, letting myself relax a little. We stood, motionless, before Noah cleared his throat.

"Paige, I know this is way too soon and isn't the way either of us planned this, but I want us to build a life together. We can make this house our own. We can have kids if that's something you want. We can make a beautiful life together."

Paco leapt from my arms and went to the kitchen to search for his new food bowl when my cell phone rang.

"Hello?" I said after putting my phone on speaker.

"I'll always find you, Petya! When I do, we will purify you of all your sins!"

I gasped and locked eyes with Noah. Neither of us needed to say a word. We both knew it was Vlad.

"You can run all you want, but that zasranets *asshole* can't keep you locked up at Thomas Hall forever. When I get you back, and I will, I'm going to beat that witchcraft out of you! I'll cleanse you of all that nonsense before you have my babies! Destroying those things in your apartment was just the first step!"

Before he could say anything more, Noah took the phone from me and ended the call. After, he powered the phone off. I should have done the same, and sooner, but after the day I'd survived, my brain was fried, and hearing Vlad's voice paralyzed me.

"You need a new number," he said, staring at the phone. It was old and obsolete, but it still worked. "And a new phone, too."

"That's not in my budget."

Before I could finish the sentence, Noah was speaking to someone on his cell. Twenty minutes later, he handed me a new one and a piece of paper with a new number.

After dinner, I sat on the sofa as Noah assembled the cat tower Vivian purchased. Paco kept climbing on Noah, using him as a cat tower instead and getting in his way.

"You're quiet. Did I scare you earlier?"

"Scare me how?"

"Talking about building a life together."

I smiled, thinking about what a wonderful a life with him would look like.

"It didn't scare me. But is that what you want? Or did you offer to marry me to keep me safe?" I asked as I closed my eyes, hoping for a particular answer.

"Open your eyes. I want you to see me say this." He said nothing more until I did so.

"You want the truth? I want everything. You, kids, the whole picket-fence dream. But I'll take anything you'll give me."

If he wanted it all, I would have to tell him everything, whether I was ready to or not. I pushed the thought away, knowing it would need to happen sooner rather than later.

"I do want a life with you," I said quietly. "And children. I gave up on the idea of being a mom ages ago."

"And?"

"You're going to make me say it, aren't you?" I asked, smiling.

"Yep," he said in a tone that accentuated his boyish grin.

"I like the idea of marrying you. Okay? And not just because of this thing with Vlad. I'm happy when we're together. For years, I looked forward to the lunches at the brewery or the Baker events I would get invited to, just so I could be near you." I sighed. "This is so much to process. Is this even real, or am I dreaming it all?"

He stood and scooped me into his arms and allowed his smile to broaden before planting his lips on mine. All worrisome thoughts left my head, and I lost myself in the deliciousness of the moment.

"Then, let's do it," he said after he pried his mouth from mine. "The sooner, the better. We'll go down to the courthouse first thing Monday morning."

Monday.

That only gave us the weekend to plan a wedding.

Not just a wedding but a life.

If I chose to stay. The idea weighed on me like a boulder on my chest. Unable to move and barely breathing. Staying was a dangerous thought, but I was beginning to care less and less about the prospect of leaving Virginia.

Chapter Eight

I NEVER WENT TO bed Friday night. I was too wired from the adrenaline that began racing through my veins after lunch. Around midnight, Noah drifted off to sleep with the sounds of soft jazz playing through the speakers in the house. Once he had, I quietly made my way to the patio with a glass of ice water and a blanket, making myself comfortable in one of the cushioned chairs perched around a glass table. Stars filled the night sky, reminding me of when Mom and I first moved to Ferma.

Thomas Hall was the nicest place I had ever been, and now I had the opportunity to live here, if I stayed. I could walk to work every day with Noah. It would be quiet and peaceful. I liked his family. There was so much love at Thomas Hall. The only thing left to do was convince myself to stay.

And I could stay if I made myself one promise. I would do anything and everything to keep Noah safe. I absolutely would not allow anything to happen to him or his family, regardless of the cost. The question was, could I put myself in harm's way if the situation arose? Because if I stayed, it certainly would.

As I sat, contemplating my future while listening to the music in the house, and the sky lightened as the sun crept toward the horizon. Daybreak was still half an hour away, but I saw Cassandra make her way along a path that ran from the pool toward our house.

Our house. It seemed like an impossible thought at the time.

"Paige, are you okay?"

"Yes, ma'am. I'm too wired to sleep. What are you doing out so early?"

"I woke early and was feeling a little restless, so I thought I'd see if anyone was up and about."

"Would you like to join me? I'd offer you tea but there's only coffee here."

"That's okay. I will have some tea sent over, though."

"Thank you. I'm not a lover of coffee myself."

"How are you feeling?" She smiled and sat. "I'm sure yesterday left you overwhelmed."

"Yes, ma'am. It has. Don't misunderstand me. I am grateful to be here. Noah has been amazing, but it's a lot to digest."

"What's been the most difficult thing? Maybe I can help."

"We haven't told anyone yet—we will later this morning—but we are getting married at the courthouse on Monday." A wave of sadness surprised me. I found myself wishing for a mother to call and share the happy news, but my mother was long lost to me. I pushed away my emotions. "This new life with Noah is going to be a big adjustment."

"Can you give me an example?"

"I'm not used to being waited on. A member of the staff delivered our dinner, set the table and cleaned the house while we ate. When I lived at the farm, I worked in the kitchen that fed everyone. It's a huge jump."

"I can only imagine. Can I ask how you and your mother ended up as part of the Orlov Cult? If you're okay talking about it."

"I don't mind."

However, she would never get the whole story.

"My real dad died when I was seven. He was a movie producer in Hollywood. We had a big house in Beverly Hills. I don't know what happened to him. I could never get anyone to tell me exactly what happened. Over the years, I've been told it was a car accident, DUI, heart attack, and drug overdose. I'll probably never know the truth. Anyway, a few years later, I came home from school one day, and Mom told me she was getting remarried and that we were moving to a large farm in the country. I was excited. I thought I'd get a stepdad who doted over me like Dad did, and if we were on a farm, I could finally get a horse and learn to ride."

"I've read enough about cults to know that it didn't turn out that way, did it?"

"No. When we got to Ferma, I had to get rid of all of my toys and clothes and wear these weird dresses with high-neck collars and long sleeves with skirts that went down to my ankles. I wasn't allowed to go to regular school either. I went to 'Farm School.' I learned to cook, sew, clean, and do other household things. Most of the girls weren't even taught to read. Those who were were only allowed to read the Bible. We were never allowed to play."

"That's terrible."

She had no clue how terrible it was. Maybe someday, I would tell the Bakers all of the gruesome details but not yet. They didn't need to know about the things Vlad did to me when I was only twelve. And how no one tried to save me.

The memory of waking up when Vlad slipped into my room in the middle of the night still haunted me. He was naked and under my sheets in seconds. At first, I didn't know what he was doing, but I knew it was wrong. His hands squeezed my barely developed breasts hard. When one hand slid down my body and between my thighs and spread my legs, I begged him to stop. That's when he covered my mouth and told me that Orlov women don't complain. They make babies for the family, which was my job now that I was a woman. His fingerprints left bruises on my body.

After that first night, I begged for help, but the only thing people did was congratulate me on becoming the newest member of Vlad's harem. That was the moment I knew I was truly, utterly alone, and the devastation was almost more than I could bear. That was when I stopped being the outgoing child who came into the family when Alexei married my mother and became the quiet, reclusive preteen who knew not to depend on anyone.

I shook those thoughts from my head and continued telling my story to Cassandra.

"When I turned sixteen, Alexei, my stepdad, announced—out of nowhere—that I would be marrying my stepbrother, Vlad, the next month. For me, it was the straw that broke the proverbial camel's back. The next morning, I packed a tote bag with my birth certificate, adoption papers, and social security card, along with a few other things. Over the years, I had removed a little money from my stepfather's wallet and squirreled it away. I had amassed close to four hundred dollars. I took the keys to one of the farm trucks and left."

"I am so sorry. I'm surprised he didn't report you missing and the truck stolen."

"I knew he would, and I'm sure he did. So, when I got to Las Vegas, I went to Walmart and bought three outfits from the clearance rack, toiletries, a backpack, and some snacks. Then, I sold the truck and bought the RAV4, which I still drive. The used car place was a little sketchy, but I think the guy knew I was escaping something major. He actually traded the farm truck for a great used car that cost three hundred dollars less so I'd have a little more cash."

"Where did you learn to drive?"

"Driving a car isn't much different than driving a tractor. I learned to do that when I was almost fourteen. Girls didn't normally get to handle the farm equipment, but one of Vlad's cousins had a crush on me. He was in charge of the trucks and tractors, so I used that to my advantage."

"You planned this for a long time, didn't you?"

"Three years. I knew I needed to look eighteen before I put the plan in place, or I'd get sent back to my family by the authorities if anything happened."

"Did you stay in Vegas?"

"No, I wasn't far enough away from California. I didn't even overnight there. I drove out to the Grand Canyon. A couple of days later, I headed towards the Florida Keys. I didn't have enough money to get there, so I went to New Orleans instead."

"A kind, elderly woman in the French Quarter caught me sleeping in my car parked in front of her shop. She fed me, and I told her my story."

"This was Miss Genevieve?" Cassandra said, half asking, half confirming.

"Yeah." Just thinking about her left a hole in my heart that ached for the loss of her. "She owned the shop, and there was a storage area above it that she wasn't using, so she found me an old bed, mini-fridge, and microwave, so I could stay there. I worked for her, cleaning the shop, waiting on customers, and that kind of thing. When I wasn't helping her, I was at the library reading."

"You enjoy reading?" I nodded. "Great! Almost everyone here loves to read. We are constantly passing books around. Noah loves suspense novels."

"Miss Genevieve liked me to tell her about the books I read. She said I was a good storyteller. Then, one day, on my lunch break, she caught me reading a book from her shop about tarot cards and taught me how to read them. She said I had 'the gift.' That it was something few people truly connected with."

While I read several books on the subject, she taught me what she knew. It was knowledge passed down from several generations in her family. I still read the cards the way she taught me, even though I had never seen her approach in my research.

"As soon as I knew everything I needed to, I started reading cards for tourists who wandered into her shop, and she let me keep the money. Miss Genevieve put an ad in one of those free tourist guides for me, and I started making good money rather quickly. She only read for her regular customers."

"Do you mind if I ask how much money you were making?"

"Usually, it was around three hundred a day."

"That's fantastic."

"Tourists are always willing to pay a little more for a French Quarter experience. I would dress in flowy broom skirts, pull my hair back with a scarf, and wear lots of jewelry. I would make my accent sound exotic and heavy. They loved it."

Cassandra smiled. She had the most beautiful smile I had ever seen.

"After about a year, I saved enough money to cut back on work hours and go to school at night for my GED. Not once would Miss Genevieve let me pay rent. She told me I was like the daughter she never had, and it was her job to take care of me. She was the mother I never had. She filled the empty hole in me that needed a mom. I wouldn't have survived without her. She meant everything to me."

My eyes filled with tears as the thought of her violent death's headline swirled in my mind.

"Why did you leave?" she asked.

I collected myself before continuing. "One morning, I was having breakfast at the diner nearby with a friend. A couple was seated at the table next to us just as we finished eating. They were friends of my stepfather. I knew they recognized me because they struck up a conversation. As soon as we left, I packed my car and drove away from Louisiana. It broke my heart to leave Miss Genevieve. I had lived above her shop for almost five years."

She reached over and took my hand, holding it tightly. Cassandra, from what I had been told, had a bizarre life before her daughters were born. She obviously understood my heartache.

"From there, I went to Nashville. I stayed in Tennessee for three years but didn't really like it. I had trouble finding people I could connect with."

"So, you moved on."

"Yep. A couple I met when I first arrived in Nashville invited me to stay with them in DC to see if I liked it. They moved to the capital six months after we met, but we kept in touch."

"I wasn't fond of Washington DC, but we came to Willow Creek for the Christmas Carnival, and I fell in love with the place. After New Year's, I drove down and went door to door in town to every business, asking if they were hiring. Zoe wasn't, but she told me the brewery was, and to tell them she sent me. It's hard to believe that was over four years ago."

"And Monday, you'll be part of the Baker family."

"I'm not sure I'm qualified to be a Baker," I replied, admitting my insecurities for the first time.

"Why do you say that?"

"Everyone here is so well educated. All I have is a GED."

"That doesn't matter."

"Says the woman with a doctorate degree."

"There are a lot of different types of intelligence. You're smart, have a lot of common sense, are well-read, and have a caring soul. Most of the time, those things are more important than a piece of paper. On top of all of that, you're resourceful, clever, determined, and brave, too."

"So, you really think it's okay that I didn't go to college?"

"Of course, if you want to go, we can make that happen, but college isn't the only means to acquire knowledge. You're already proof of that."

"Really?"

"Yes, really. The Baker family can do anything. I wasn't always a Baker. It took a while to understand what the name means. Once you do, you'll understand how amazing your life can be."

"You know, she'll technically be a Foster," Noah said. His mother's maiden name was Baker.

I turned to see Noah standing on the threshold of the open patio door. He was shirtless, with his sleep pants hanging low on his hips. My eyes traced his well-defined abs, and my mouth watered. No man had ever solicited that kind of response from me, and I was taken aback by my reaction.

I bit my bottom lip, admiring his Adonis-like body. "What if I want to stay a Wilson?"

"Do you?" he asked, raising an eyebrow.

Cassandra grinned before looking at the time on her phone. "I think I'm going to head home before Colin wakes up and starts worrying about me."

I stood, and she gave me a long hug. "Welcome to the family."

"Thank you for listening."

"I know I'm not your mother, but if you ever need a mom to talk to, you know where to find me."

I nodded and pushed back happy tears.

Noah stepped onto the patio and gave his aunt a quick hug before holding me as we watched Cassandra walk away.

"Will you keep your last name?"

"I don't know. Wilson was my dad's last name. When my step-dad adopted me, it was changed to Orlov. I kind of like Foster, though. Maybe I'll keep Wilson as my middle name. Paige Wilson Foster. Paige W. Foster. Yeah, I like that."

Chapter Nine

ONCE CASSANDRA WAS OUT of sight, I walked into the house, and Noah followed. The sliding glass door was off the den, so I dropped myself onto the sofa. Noah sat as well. It only took him a fraction of a second to wrap me in his arms and pull me close to him. It dawned on me that, in the last twenty-four hours, whenever we were in the same room, he had his hands somewhere on my body, or I was wrapped in his arms. After spending most of my adult life alone and having little physical affection as a child, it was strange to be physically attached to another person.

"I don't think I've ever realized what a touchy-feely person you are."

Noah tilted his head to get a better look at me. "I'm not."

I looked at his arms.

"All evidence to the contrary."

He leaned in and laid two perfect kisses on my neck. "Okay, I'm usually not. But ever since our run-in with Vlad, whenever I am within eyeshot of you, I think about how you glued yourself to me for safety outside the diner. I want you to always feel that safe."

I smiled, and he continued.

"And it's a good excuse to touch your soft, alabaster skin and play with your hair. It would seem you have turned me into a constant contact kind of guy."

I closed my eyes and let my body melt into his. The next thing I remembered was Noah's hand cupping my cheek.

I opened my eyes before he spoke.

"Babe, I hate to wake you, but we are needed at Gran's."

"Why?" I sat up.

"Wedding arrangements. You need to make some decisions."

"About what?"

"Everything."

After a quick shower, I brushed my teeth and hair before I dressed in the same clothes I wore the day before. I had nothing else to wear.

Noah and I walked the path to the main house, taking our time.

"Are you sure about this?" I asked.

"About what?"

"Getting married."

He smiled as he pulled closer. "It was my idea, remember?"

It was his idea, and as much as I liked it, I wasn't sure if it was a smart one.

We were met at the door by Miss Vivian, Phoebe, and Faith. Classical music quietly played in the background. I had been to the main house before, but there had never been music playing unless there was a party, and I was thankful for it. After greetings and hugs, we were guided into a formal sitting room. Faith joined us, but Miss Vivian and Phoebe continued down the hall.

The sitting room had been converted into a jewelry store. Cases of rings, earrings, bracelets, and necklaces covered folding tables covered with linen tablecloths. An elderly man, probably close to eighty, with white hair and a limp, was wandering around putting the last few items out.

"I don't understand," I said as I stared at an exquisite pair of diamond and pearl drop earrings in a velvet box on the closest table.

"You need to pick out an engagement ring, and we need to look at wedding bands," Noah said.

"How did this all end up here? I only told Cassandra about our engagement a few hours ago."

Noah didn't hesitate before speaking.

"She probably called Aunt Zoe, who called Gran, and poof! Welcome to the Baker women who run Thomas Hall."

"Okay," I said hesitantly. "I get the rings, but what about everything else?"

"Well, you'll need accessories to go with whatever you decide to wear," Faith added. "Aunt Zoe is setting up a boutique down the hall with dresses."

My breathing grew shallow, and lightheadedness overtook my ability to focus. I dropped into a nearby antique upholstered chair and lowered my head to my knees. Instantly, Noah was beside me.

"Babe, breathe. You're okay." I turned my head to see his smiling face. "It's time to plan our wedding and become part of the Baker clan."

I slowly sat up and gazed at Faith, who was standing next to Noah. "Help me."

"I know this seems like a lot," said the jeweler with a kind, deep voice. "Let me help you eliminate some things. Tell me your favorite gem shapes."

"Um, square or rectangle." The jeweler scurried around, eliminating over half of the rings.

As he did, the three of us relocated to one of the many sofas in the room.

"Okay, square or emerald cut. What else do I need to know?"

"Nothing under three carats," Noah commented, and the jeweler cut the number of rings by over half again.

As he did, I turned to Noah. "Isn't that a lot? I don't need anything that big."

"You're worth every penny and then some." He smiled and kissed my temple.

"Noah," I whispered with a shaky voice and teary eyes.

A tray of rings was placed in my lap, and I was instructed to pull any I liked. I was chewing on my bottom lip before I picked three. The process was repeated four more times, and the rings I chose were then put on a single tray. Completely overwhelmed, I eliminated a couple before handing the tray to Noah.

"I can't decide. You choose."

He and Faith reviewed the possibilities together, had me try on a few rings, and narrowed it down to two. I picked up my favorite and handed it to Noah.

"This one," I said with a smile.

"Nice choice," the jeweler commented. "It's a Platinum Pavé Antique Clover Ring with a three-and-a-half-carat emerald diamond in the center."

Silently, Noah slid off his seat and onto one knee, holding the ring in front of me.

"Oh, Noah. That's not necessary."

"Of course it is. Paige, do you have a middle name?" I slowly shook my head. My eyes were locked with his. "Paige Wilson, will you do me the honor of becoming my wife?"

I glanced over at Faith, who was smiling and staring at her own recently received ring, before turning my attention to the man in front of me.

"Yes, yes, I will marry you."

Despite knowing I should've been running away, that it would be safer that way for the Baker family, I was done fighting my feelings. I was tired of running from the Orlov cult. It was time to stand my ground and fight for the life I deserved. I just prayed I wouldn't regret the decision.

He slid the ring onto my finger, but it was two sizes too big.

The jeweler picked up the phone, muttered a few words, and then swiftly approached us. He removed the ring and measured my finger size.

"As soon as you pick your wedding bands, I'll have the rings taken to town and properly sized. They'll be back later tonight."

Choosing wedding bands was easier. Noah wanted them to be platinum and engraved with a design. It didn't really matter to me. So, when the jeweler pulled out the matching set of thick platinum bands with grapevines engraved on them, the search was over. They weren't necessarily my first choice, but I liked them, and they were Noah's favorite.

Faith smiled. "Those are perfect. Say goodbye to Noah. Time for dresses."

"I thought he could give me his opinion on that as well."

A sharp "no" left Faith's mouth. "Don't you know it's bad luck for the groom to see the dress ahead of time?"

"I'll stay here and fill out paperwork and see you back in here when you know what accessories you need," Noah said as he pulled me from the sofa and helped me to my feet.

I gave him a soft kiss on the lips and let him hold me. "Thank you, Noah. The rings are beautiful."

"Not as beautiful as you."

Faith placed her hand on my arm, and I released my grip around his neck. Faith and I interlocked arms and left the room, heading down the hall to the library.

"I can't believe this is happening," I said as I turned to Faith. "It's like I've stepped into a dream."

I just prayed Vlad wouldn't turn it into a nightmare.

She smiled as she led me through the library door.

The room's furniture had been rearranged, and the space had been converted into a wedding boutique. Dresses, shoes, cocktail bags, and undergarments covered every available space, minus a path around the space.

I stood in the doorway, mouth ajar. Faith guided me to the sofa where Miss Vivian and Phoebe were sitting.

Miss Vivian picked up my left hand and frowned. "No ring?"

"There is, but it's too large to stay on my finger. The jeweler is having it resized. It should be back tonight."

Phoebe turned to Faith while Miss Vivian continued to hold my hand and pat the top of it.

"How is it?" Phoebe asked.

"Excellent, my cousin has excellent taste. He didn't go cheap, either. Platinum, three-and-a-half carat emerald cut diamond, clover-shaped setting. It's gorgeous."

As Faith described the ring to Phoebe, I scanned the room at the dozens of dresses hanging in front of me.

"Where do I even begin in here?" I asked them both after Faith finished the description of the rings.

"That's easy! At the beginning," a sassy voice said from between two racks of clothing.

Zoe appeared and made her way to me.

Zoe Marshall, Henry's common-law wife, was a gorgeous woman with a tawny complexion and straight black hair. For years, her hair had been nearly waist-length, but just before the holidays the year prior, she had it cut into a long bob. The newer look suited her and, in my opinion, made her look younger.

"Do you have any thoughts?" Zoe asked.

"Well, it's a courthouse wedding. Maybe I should wear a simple dress or suit. I don't want anything long or too formal."

Zoe and Phoebe scrunched their faces, and Miss Vivian's lips made a tight line. Was I wrong to think something simple was best? I knew how expensive these dresses could be. I had no idea how I was going to pay for it, and only a dozen people would probably ever see it.

Faith gave the women a decisive side eye before speaking up in my defense.

"Sounds wonderful. Aunt Zoe can find something fabulous, I'm sure."

Zoe moved through the room, pulling dress bags. When she returned, she unzipped the bags and showed me their contents. When she was done, I had four options to try.

After very little debate, I chose a white sleeveless tea-length sheath dress with a matching long swing coat that needed no alterations. It was simple, classic and perfect—until I looked at the price tag.

"Stop doing that. The dress is a gift from me," Zoe said.

"I can't let you do that."

"You can, and you will," Zoe said in her usual, sassy tone.

"But it's—it's—"

"A wedding dress," Zoe said, swatting my hand away from the tag. "It's okay to spend a few thousand on it. Besides, you are right. It's the perfect style for a courthouse elopement."

After choosing the dress, I had to decide on everything else. I tried on three pairs of shoes before Phoebe brought over a pair of white Louboutin heels. I had spotted them earlier, but those iconic red soles were more expensive than three month's rent at my old apartment, so I steered clear. When I slid them on my feet, I immediately understood why people were willing to spend that kind of money on shoes.

After that, the bejeweled cocktail bag and short white gloves were quickly decided on, giving the look a sixties retro vibe. When the women saw the look, they gave approving smiles.

"I love it! It's the ideal look for a courthouse wedding," Faith said.

Zoe stated as she circled me, "I thought it wasn't the right one when I pulled it from the rack, but it's you. It's perfect, especially with the shoes."

"Almost perfect. I'll be right back," Noah's grandmother said.

Vivian left the room and returned with a few necklaces, bracelets, and earrings from the jeweler. I chose the pearl drop earrings I had seen earlier but decided against a necklace. Faith went into the jewelry room and found the perfect bracelet, so I went with that instead.

When we were done, there was an early tea of finger sandwiches, scones, fruit, and sweets awaiting us in the sunroom. Noah and I snuggled on an oversized chaise after we ate and ended up napping away the afternoon in Miss Vivian's sunroom.

A while later, I stirred when I heard two people talking. I didn't open my eyes but listened. It only took me a minute to realize it was Noah and his mom.

"She looked exhausted when we were picking out her dress. I'm glad she's getting some rest," Phoebe said in a hushed voice.

"I don't think she slept last night," Noah replied.

"Can you blame her? It sounds like her family is full of psychopaths. She's taken so much effort to remain hidden from them, yet they keep hunting her down."

"I think there is a lot more to the story that we don't know yet. She tried to tell me something the night of our first date, but I stopped her. I wonder now if that was a mistake."

"Well, it can't be anything worse than what we already know."

"I think it might be."

"Are you sure you want to do this? Paige is a wonderful girl, Noah, but I'm worried for your safety."

A pang of guilt filled my body, knowing I was causing Phoebe to worry for her son.

His fingers combed through my straw-colored hair.

"Yeah. I've never been more positive about anything in my life. It's like we're magnets, drawn to one another. Ever since Hope and Grayson's wedding, if I'm not with her, I can't think. Hell, I can't breathe. She is everything, Mom."

The sentiment was overwhelming. Before Phoebe could say anything else, I shifted in his arms and opened my eyes. He looked at me and smiled.

"Hi, beautiful. Did you sleep well?"

"I did," I said, sitting up and smoothing my hair as I spoke. "I can't believe I fell asleep here, though. I must find your grandmother and apologize at once."

Phoebe chimed in. She was sitting in a chair across from us.

"No, she was thrilled you felt comfortable enough here to rest after lunch."

"It's a relaxing place to be. But if I don't do something soon, though, I might doze back off."

Phoebe laughed as she stood, patting both Noah and me on the head as she left the room. When she did, Noah rolled his eyes.

"Why don't we go for a walk before it gets dark?" he asked.

"Great idea," I replied as I stood. "You know, I've never seen the entire estate before."

"Well then, let's do that. But if you want to see everything before the sun sets, we'll need to grab a golf cart instead."

Noah and I cut through the kitchen, where the staff was busy preparing for dinner. The chef stopped me and asked if I preferred lamb or pork chops for the evening meal. It was strange to live in a world where I wasn't required to cook every night, let alone have a choice of what I would be served. I liked both, so I left the decision to the chef.

On exiting the house by way of the kitchen door, a small fleet of golf carts, all recently repainted purple with the new Thomas Hall logo embossed on the side.

We hopped into the first one in line, and Noah took me to parts of the estate I hadn't seen before. Storage barns, dorms for the field hands, and the winemaster's house were all pointed out to me.

The white farm-style home belonged to Alex, Noah's uncle, and his wife, Libby. While Faith was also a winemaster there, she was currently juggling her time between Cassandra's house at Thomas Hall, where she grew up, and Ben's apartment in town, all while renovating a historic Victorian home in Willow Creek.

At the edge of the property, a tall fence marked the boundary with driving paths on both sides. Beyond the estate, a forest created a curtain of pines.

A cool sweat coated the back of my neck, and my breathing became labored.

Noah stopped the cart.

"Paige, babe, are you okay? You're as white as a ghost."

"It's just that—that the fence reminds me of Ferma."

Noah didn't say a word but quickly drove the cart away from the fence. As he did, I thought I saw a person standing at the edge of the forest, staring at us.

"Oh my god! Someone is out there."

"Where?" Noah asked.

I had turned and faced him, but when I looked back to the woods, the person was gone.

"They're gone. Whoever it was was built like Vlad, but I'm not sure it was him. Or maybe I just imagined it."

As soon as we pulled up to our house, Noah wrapped me in his arms and whispered in my ear, "Babe, you're safe here."

I wanted to believe him, but I feared his overconfidence was a delusion created from the fear of me running from Thomas Hall.

The insulated estate made it easy to be lulled into Noah's false sense of security.

He held me until the sun dropped beyond the horizon. When he released me, he smiled as he looked at me and said, "Come on. Let's get you a glass of wine."

Chapter Ten

AFTER A SPECTACULAR DINNER of lamb chops with mint jelly and sautéed squash sent down from the main house, Noah and I sat on the sofa in our den, each enjoying a third glass of wine. It was time for a discussion I didn't want to have with Noah but needed to. I debated the best way to begin when Noah's voice broke me out of my inner monologue.

"What is it you don't want to tell me?"

"Am I really that easy to read?"

"Sometimes. This time, I see it in your eyes. There's something you don't want to talk about but feel like you need to tell me. My guess is that it's about your past."

Tears welled, and I wanted to say something, anything, but the words were caught in my throat, so I looked away. I couldn't look at him and tell him about this part of my life.

His hand cupped my face and moved it until we were eye to eye. "It's that bad, huh?"

I nodded.

He stood, lit a candle on the opposite side of the room, turned the music from eighties classics to soft piano music, then killed the lights.

"Turn the music off."

"Really?"

"Yes, I don't want this associated with anything more than it already is."

He followed my directions before returning to the sofa, where he positioned us, so that my back was pressed against his chest, and his arms were around me. After throwing a blanket over us, he handed me a tissue.

"Okay. It's about sex."

"Okay."

"I want to be a good wife to you. The best wife. But I need you to know, before we say 'I do' that I'll probably never enjoy having sex."

"Why?"

I sat for a long moment. This was the part I didn't want to talk about.

"When I was young, my stepbrother used to crawl into my bed at night. He would"—I inhaled and swallowed hard—"do things."

Every muscle in Noah's body went solid.

"How young?"

"I was twelve. Almost thirteen. I had my first period two weeks earlier, so Alexei, my stepdad, decided it was time for me to start making babies. For the good of the family."

"Wait a minute. Your stepdad told your stepbrother to impregnate you? So, he raped you? That's fucked up."

"Yeah."

"How old was Vlad then? He looked a lot older than you when I saw him."

"He was twenty-six the first time it happened."

"Jesus."

"I went to my stepdad the next morning. He told me the same thing Vlad had said. When I went to my mom, she told me I had to do as I was told and listen to the men."

"But why would they want you to start having babies so young? I mean, couldn't they have waited until you were an adult? Wasn't there a way for you to call the police?"

I hadn't expected Noah to have so many questions, and it caused my stress to soar.

I took a deep breath and blew it out. "Noah, there are no phones at Ferma to call anyone. And even if I could call for help, Ferma is a religious community. The local police never wanted to get involved. As for starting so young, as a woman in a cult, the more babies you had, the more tied you are to the community. You aren't going to leave if you have no way to provide for your children, and if you feel that strongly about leaving, you wouldn't leave them behind."

"Oh," he muttered, dumbfounded.

"The next time, I tried to fight back. When I screamed, my stepfather came in and smacked me. Then he told Vlad he was a failure. He showed Vlad what to do by raping me after he beat me into silence."

The tears I had been trying to hold in dripped down my face. This was the first time I had ever told this story in this much detail, and I had no idea how he would react.

"How long?"

His voice was flat. I was glad it was dark so I wouldn't have to see his expression.

"My stepfather, only twice. I quickly learned that if I didn't scream at Vlad, he wouldn't come in and do it. And he was more violent than Vlad."

"And your stepbrother?"

"A couple of times a month until I ran away. So, three years. I don't know how, but I never got pregnant."

"It always happened at night?" He half-asked, half stated.

"Uh-huh."

"And that's why you can't tolerate the silence."

I nodded.

"I'm going to kill the son of a bitch." His voice was low and gravelly. It was a tone I had never heard from him before. "Both of them. I will find them, and they will die."

Neither of us said anything more until the silence was maddening, so I spoke.

"If you don't want to marry me, knowing what you now know, I would understand." I braced myself, knowing most men would not want to take on that kind of baggage.

"This changes nothing for us, Paige. Do you understand? Nothing." He paused, and I nodded. "Have you had sex since?"

"A couple of times with a guy I dated in Nashville. He told me I was a dead fish in bed. The relationship didn't last long after he said that. I really wanted to learn to like it, but it was numbing for me. I spent so many years dissociating while Vlad was on top of me that I don't know how to do it any other way."

"Stand up," he said, and I did as I was told. He stood, grabbed my hand, and guided me up the stairs. When we neared the bedroom door, he dropped my hand. "Get ready for bed. I forgot to blow out the candle and lock up. I'll be back."

I was on the last step of my nighttime routine when I heard Noah in the backyard repeatedly screaming, "She did not fucking deserve this!"

I stood and walked over to the window, where I watched him talk to himself as he paced. I knew he would be upset with the knowledge of my past life, but I found the intensity of his emotions overwhelming.

I returned to the edge of the bed I had been sitting on, holding my head in my hands, until Noah entered the room. He was seemingly calm yet had red eyes and a blotchy face. He sat on the edge of the bed, picking up the hairbrush I had dropped when I heard him scream.

He began to talk as he finished brushing my hair and then braided it.

"If you really want this part of a marriage, I have an idea. But if you don't, I understand. We can adopt kids. There are dozens of ways to make a family."

"I want us to try. If we are going to be married, I want us to be completely married. I want us to have a normal, loving marriage."

"And what do you think that looks like?"

His question caught me off guard. I had no clue what normal looked like, especially when it came to marriage, so I turned his question back on him.

"What do you think a good marriage should be?"

"My parents divorced when I was young, so definitely not like theirs. Probably a marriage like Aunt Cassie and Uncle Edward had. They were so happy together."

"What happened to him? I know he died not too long after I moved here, but that's all."

"He had his third heart attack at sixty-eight and died. They built the gazebo near the spot where it happened."

"Oh. So, what did they do that was so special?"

"From what I saw as a kid, they always moved through life together. They were a team. But if they ever had an issue, they would talk about it, find a compromise that worked for both of them, and move forward, making sure their pace matched their partner. And that's what we are going to do. We are going to go slow. I want you to be comfortable with me, for you to set the pace, and to be one hundred percent ready of every stage of our life together. That includes sex. I want us both to enjoy ourselves, and I want you to stop me the second you don't feel good about something."

"Okay."

"I think we have a good start. Correct me if I'm wrong, but you seem to like me kissing you, holding you, and being near you."

I felt the care and compassion in his voice.

I nodded as he brushed away a stray hair from my face. "That is a fine start. Isn't it?"

Noah smiled. "What do you want to try next?"

"I want to sleep next to you. I don't want to be alone knowing Vlad is out there."

"Babe, you're safe at Thomas Hall. It's always been secure. My Uncle Edward saw to that when Aunt Cassandra moved here. He turned the place into a fortress. And after what happened with Hope, we made some upgrades. There's no way anyone can get to you."

Late the previous summer, Hope's stalker had infiltrated the Baker compound. He only stopped pursuing her when Hope shot and killed him after he attacked her bodyguard in an attempt to get close to her.

"So, you don't want me to sleep in your bed knowing what you now know?"

It didn't happen often anymore, but over the course of the evening, the shame of what happened to me had been building and spilled over with the question.

"Oh, no, babe. You are sleeping next to me tonight and every night unless you change your mind, no matter what." He pulled back the comforter and top sheet. "I just want you to know that you are safe."

His words dissipated my shame, and I made my way into the bed.

"Noah, if the last two days have proved anything, I know I will always be safe when I'm with you."

I might have been fooling myself, but for the first time in my adult life, I felt safe, and I wasn't about to run from a feeling like that.

Noah leaned in and kissed me softly at first. When I applied more pressure to his lips, he followed. Before long, we were stretched across the bed in a tangle of arms and legs. His lips only left mine to meander along my jawline and neck. They found themselves in my cleavage on more than one occasion.

I never thought I would be able to feel comfortable in bed with a man. I was wrong. Noah's presence was the most natural thing in the world.

Over forty minutes later and still fully dressed, we were staring at each other. He had the most beautiful eyes, shining as he smiled at me.

"Let's get some rest, beautiful."

I nodded, but I didn't want to sleep.

I wanted to enjoy the moment—a moment I thought I would never have with a man so kind and loving, and I knew I didn't deserve him because he deserved more. He should have been with someone less broken and someone who brought less danger to his life, but I was going to hold on to him for as long as I could.

Wrapped in his arms, I drifted off to sleep.

Chapter Eleven

I WOKE UP SUNDAY morning alone in bed, with the sun blasting through the windows. It was only seven-thirty, so I was surprised to discover I was alone in the house.

I made my way to the kitchen. The water for my tea had just begun to bubble when I heard the gravel crunch under a car's tires and the front door open.

"Noah? Is that you?"

"Yeah," he said, making his way to the kitchen to join me. He smiled, but his expression seemed forced.

After pouring the water over my loose tea and leaving it to steep, I walked to Noah and wrapped my arms around his waist. Now that I was close to him, I could see the dark circles under his eyes and the haggard expression he was trying to hide.

"What's wrong?"

"Nothing."

"Try again. You're a terrible liar."

Noah sucked in a deep breath before dropping onto one of the tall chairs at the breakfast bar. "Really, it's nothing."

"No, tell me. We can tell each other anything. Everything. Right?"

With his hands on my hips, he pulled me close until I was between his legs.

"I woke up in the middle of the night. I couldn't fall back asleep and started thinking about everything you told me."

I tried to step away from his grasp, knowing he had to be repulsed by what I shared with him the previous night, but he held me tight.

"Don't. This isn't about you. I mean, obviously, it is. But it's not. The more I thought about it all, the angrier I got. I wanted to fucking kill Vlad. And that asshole stepfather of yours as well."

Had he done it? Had he killed the man who destroyed my innocence? My expression must have matched my thoughts.

"No, babe. I didn't kill the son of a bitch. I went for a drive instead. I do that when there's a lot on my mind."

"Oh," I said, lowering my tone in hopes he would find it soothing. "Did it help?"

"Some." Noah paused as though waiting on me. When I said nothing, he continued. "Aren't you going to ask me where I went?"

"Should I? Does it matter?"

"It's just most women I've dated get suspicious and want to know where the fuck I've been."

I stepped back, tilted my head, and put my hands on my hips.

Noah raised his eyebrows, and I rolled my eyes.

"Noah, am I anything like most women you've dated?"

Having never met anyone he dated, I didn't know for sure, but I had a good idea.

He shook his head.

"If going for a drive is your thing to ease your tension, I won't ask questions. And I can tell by your language you are stressed. If you want me to know where you've gone, you'll have to tell me. Okay?"

He inhaled a deep breath and leaned into me until we were nose to nose. "I'm sorry about the swearing. I know it's something you don't normally do, and you don't deserve to have to listen to that."

"It's okay. I know it's not about me."

"I will tell you this. Somehow, someway, I'm going to make Vlad and his father pay for everything they did to you."

I shifted to lay my head on his shoulder, and he held me until his stomach growled.

I separated myself from him and, wanting to change the subject, said, "It sounds like it's time to make some breakfast."

After breakfast, Noah decided we should rearrange the house. Since it was meant to be ours and not his mother's home, he wanted it to reflect our preferences, not hers. This meant making decisions. As Noah knew, from our first date, I froze when overwhelmed with options.

However, we took things room by room and by the middle of the afternoon. We were tired and sweaty from moving furniture but had everything where we liked it. The nicknacks and a few pieces of furniture, along with several pictures that we didn't care for, had been picked up by the staff and stored elsewhere.

We were sitting on the sofa in the den, drinking lemonade, when the doorbell rang.

"I'll get it," Noah said as he stood and made his way to the door.

I couldn't see who it was but recognized the voice. It was Miss Vivian.

"Oh, I love the way you and Paige have moved things around. It's so much more open."

I stood when they entered the den. However, at the same time, I could hear people rattling around in the kitchen and dining room.

"Hi," I said as Miss Vivian made her way to me and grabbing my hand.

"I want to see the ring," she said, and I smiled as I showed it off to her.

"You couldn't wait a few hours until dinner?" Noah asked.

"Oh, you two don't want to deal with the family tonight. Anyway, you'll see them all tomorrow after the courthouse at brunch. That's why I had some of the kitchen staff come with me. They've brought dinner and are setting the table. All you'll have to do is put it in the oven for an hour before you want to eat."

"Thank you," I mumbled.

I wasn't used to being pampered like this. It was a lot to take in.

"Any time. Now, while I'm here, let's finalize the menu for tomorrow."

The three of us sat on the sofa, and she opened a small notebook she had been holding.

"So, here's what I'm thinking. We'll do this buffet style. Fruit and cheese, of course. I thought a spinach and mandarin salad would be nice unless you prefer something else."

"No," I said. "That's fine."

I could feel Noah's eyes on me, knowing if he bombarded me with choices, I'd get overwhelmed.

"Since we are doing brunch, quiche is a must. What's your favorite kind?"

"I don't know. Whatever you think is fine."

Vivian patted my knee. "It's your wedding brunch. I want you to have what you like."

My pulse raced as my nervousness grew.

"Noah?" I whispered, and he moved from the other side of his grandmother and sat next to me, wrapping an arm around me.

"Gran, why don't you go with the Quiche Lorraine? Everyone loves that." He turned to me. "Gruyère and bacon."

I nodded.

"Paige gets a little overwhelmed with too many choices, Gran."

"Oh, well, let's try a different approach. I'll tell you my thoughts, and you tell me if you want me to change anything."

"Okay," I said, feeling more at ease.

Vivian went on to tell me her idea of the perfect brunch, and when we were done, we had a menu that included salad and quiche, as well as salmon, herb-crusted potatoes with onions, avocado toast, Nutella-filled crepes, and a small wedding cake.

After Vivian left, Noah knew I was a nervous wreck without me saying a word. So, he drew me a bath, changed the music from eighties pop to soft, classical, romantic music and got dinner in the oven while I soaked.

Noah and I were snuggled together in bed Sunday night, listening to the rain beat on the windowpanes. The night before, I discovered that Noah liked to spoon. Having never slept next to a man, I didn't know it, but I did, too.

"You're quiet tonight. Getting cold feet?" he asked.

"No."

"But?"

"Have we lost our minds? I mean, think about all we've decided in the last seventy-two hours. Friday morning, we had only been on one date, and now we are getting married in the morning. I'm still not sure this is the right thing. Vlad is going to come after you."

"Babe," he said, pulling me closer. "You're just nervous. I won't let Vlad touch us. I promise. This is going to be great. Okay?"

"Okay."

My voice wavered. I wanted to tell him he had no clue the lengths Vlad would go to get me back to Ferma, but there was no point in ruining Noah's confidence. However, the heavy burden of knowing what the Baker family refused to see would slowly drive me mad.

Noah could tell something was bothering me. He thought he knew what it was.

"Paige, are you regretting not having a big wedding?"

"No, the courthouse is fine. My dream was a small beach wedding, but I like the idea of a simple ceremony and the family meal Miss Vivian is planning afterward. It's so much less stressful than something like Hope's wedding."

"When all of this is over, we'll take a honeymoon trip somewhere tropical. Maybe Bermuda? The family has a beachfront place there."

"That sounds heavenly. I'll have to get a passport."

Chapter Twelve

MONDAY MORNING, I WOKE with the weight of Noah's arm across me. I liked waking up next to him, feeling safe and loved. Even though we had never said it to one another, we loved each other. His actions over the last three days proved his love for me that I had for him in return.

The clock on the bedside table read five-forty-three. We were leaving for City Hall at nine. So, I slid out from under Noah's arm and quickly made my way to the shower.

Twenty minutes later, I emerged in a white satin robe Gran brought me Saturday afternoon with clean hair, shaved legs, and brushed teeth. The bed was empty.

I made my way downstairs and found a note on the kitchen table.

> *Paige,*
> *Went for a quick run with Colin & Henry.*
> *Be back by 8:00.*
> *Can't wait to be your husband!*
> *Noah*

I pulled a bottle of water from the fridge and had just taken the first sip from it when there was a knock at the door. I was only halfway to it when it opened. Zoe paraded in with a large makeup case and two other girls from her shop.

"Happy wedding day!" she exclaimed.

"Good morning. I didn't know you were coming over this morning."

"Did you really think I would let you get married at City Hall looking anything less than fabulous?"

Zoe's Spa & Boutique was the place to go for hair, nails, facials, makeup, and fantastic clothes. She was the reason the Baker women always looked stylish. In the past, her store was out of my budget. Whenever I saw her, though, she would always find something about my wardrobe to sincerely compliment. The color of my blouse, stacked necklaces, and shoes were kindly spoken about.

Every Christmas, Henry gave me a gift certificate to her shop. Zoe made it go as far as possible, having lived on a tight budget at various points in her life, and claimed everything I picked out was on sale.

Before I could answer Zoe, there was another knock on the door. This time, it was Miss Vivian, Phoebe, and Noah's older sister Nora. Members of the kitchen staff followed them with breakfast trays. One carried a large white box with a purple ribbon.

"Brides never remember to eat," Miss Vivian casually commented.

"And there is no way I'm letting my new daughter get ready alone," Phoebe said while giving me a big hug.

"I have responsibilities as your soon-to-be sister to make sure everything goes smoothly." Nora smiled. "I've always wanted a sister."

I hugged Nora, and before I could close the door, Cassandra, with her daughters Hope, Faith, and Joy, arrived, carrying bottles of champagne. Hope had returned from her honeymoon late the night before, so I was surprised to see her and greeted her with a hug as well.

"Oh my god! I leave for a week and come home to you and Noah getting married. Let me see the ring!"

I showed her the ring, and Faith and Joy leaned in for a look as well.

"Aunt Zoe," Faith said. "Please tell me Paige is starting with a manicure."

"Her nails look fine," Hope replied.

"They are still that God-awful pink you insisted on for your bridesmaids."

Hope rolled her eyes.

"Don't worry. I'm going to change out the color to a gel French manicure."

This was all becoming overwhelming quickly, causing my head to swirl.

"I think I need a drink."

"Good," Joy said, kissing my cheek, "because you can't get ready without champagne. It's tradition."

My eyes filled with tears, but I fought them back. I was wrong when I told Cassandra during our early-morning talk on Saturday that none of my family would be with me on my wedding day. This was my family now. And it was a magnificent one.

And just when I thought it couldn't get any more perfect, the doorbell rang.

Joy answered it, and Libby walked in with a bouquet of flowers.

"Sorry I took so long. I had to run into town to pick up your bouquet and Noah's boutonniere from the florist. I hope you like it. It's your wedding gift from Alex and me."

The bouquet was a gorgeous arrangement of white lilies, roses, and baby's breath tied with a white satin ribbon. Noah's boutonniere consisted of a single white rosebud.

By the time Noah returned from his run, the dining room and kitchen were abuzz with activity. At first, I didn't know who had arrived, only that the front door had opened.

Then I heard his voice.

"Wow! What a party! Has anyone seen my bride?"

"I'm in the dining room."

"It's bad luck to see the bride before the wedding!" his grandmother said, trying to block the doorway.

"Too late, Gran. I woke up at three this morning and stared at her for about twenty minutes, and I peeked at her in the shower this morning." He gave her a hug and slowly turned, pivoting her out of his way.

By the time he was done talking, he was on his knees next to me, and Zoe was finishing my hair. What followed was a spectacular kiss. While my nails and makeup had already been done, Zoe had waited to put on lipstick, so I could continue eating and drinking, not worried about it smearing.

"You look so beautiful," he whispered, pulling his lips away from mine. "Did you open your gift?"

I looked over at the box. "No, I was waiting until you got back."

He grabbed the box and placed it in my lap.

I had a good idea of what it was. When the bridesmaids were getting ready for Hope's wedding, there was a great discussion of brides receiving white fur coats from their Baker husbands.

I untied the ribbon and lifted the top. I was right.

"Noah, it's lovely." I stood as I lifted it, letting the box fall to the floor.

As soon as it did, my mind flashed back to a Christmas long ago. It was the last Christmas my father was still alive. He had been insistent that my mom and I open our presents at the same time. When we did, they were matching tan fur jackets. They were very popular in L.A. at the time.

As quickly as the memory flashed into my brain, it was gone, and I was teary-eyed. When I blinked, I found myself face-to-face with Noah.

"Babe, are you okay?"

"Yeah, I was just thinking about my dad. I wish he were here."

Noah gave me a long, tight hug before he helped me slip the new coat on over my robe. It was a little big, but I liked my coats that way. It was soft and warm but lighter in weight than I expected.

"It may be too warm to wear it today. But that's up to you."

My dress already had a matching swing coat, so I knew this present would stay in the closet. I gave Noah a big hug. "Thank you. But I feel bad. I didn't get you anything."

"You're welcome, babe. But don't feel bad. You're all I need, and I'm about to get you for a lifetime." He gave me another tight squeeze before letting me go. "I'm going to go upstairs and get ready. Send the guys up when they get here."

I didn't ask who he was referring to. If the Baker women arrived unannounced, the men would undoubtedly follow. And I was right. By the time Noah and I were dressed and ready to walk out the door, every member of the Baker family was in our house.

Chapr Thirteen

T HE CLOCK IN THE courthouse lobby read ten-twenty as we walked out of its oversized front doors. The bright sunlight momentarily blinded us.

Once we could see again, white rose petals were falling around us like giant snowflakes making their way to Earth. There wasn't much doubt in my mind that Noah's Aunt Libby arranged for rose petals when she picked up my bouquet.

The Baker family had followed us and waited on the steps, along with my neighbors, John and Jake, as well as a few coworkers from the brewery. Passersby also stopped to watch, including Mrs. Lowenstein and her dog, Baxter.

Miss Vivian hired a photographer who took pictures at the house while I was getting ready and followed us to the courthouse.

Noah leaned in and kissed me. The camera's lens's shutter clicked as my mouth melted into his. This was the magic moment every girl dreamt about, and while I hadn't, this was heaven.

This was everything.

And it was happening to me.

We only broke our kiss and opened our eyes when we heard a raucous. The photographer was sprawled across the steps of the courthouse, her head bleeding onto the concrete, and Vlad was standing behind her with a gun pointed in our direction.

"Did you really think you could take what is MINE?"

Noah's lightbulb moment concerning Vlad indicated he finally understood what I had been trying to tell him all along. Vlad was batshit, next-level crazy.

I knew what was about to happen. As Vlad aimed to fire his gun, I stepped in front of Noah, not thinking twice about protecting him.

Time slowed to a crawl, and when I peered down, blood seeped onto my white dress. There was a moment before I comprehended that it was my blood and was shocked that it didn't hurt. Everything my body was doing seemed to be in slow motion as I stared at the crimson liquid. It spread, and a burning sensation flared in my left hip and torso. That's when my legs gave out from under me, and Noah's strong arms lowered me to the ground.

This was how I would die, but I was at peace with that, knowing Noah was safe. And with me gone, the Orlovs would leave the Bakers alone.

I had misread Noah's cards. He wasn't going to die. Someone he cared for would.

The voices around me seemed far away and became more hushed with each second. It was hard to tell who was who, but occasionally, Noah's voice broke through.

"Stay with me, Paige. Help is coming. Stay with me, babe."

As my vision and hearing faded, I needed Noah to know one thing, so I managed to mumble, "Noah, I love you."

Chapter Fourteen

I OPENED MY EYES to fluorescent lights, not knowing where I was or how I had gotten there. The last thing I remembered was being at the courthouse with white rose petals falling around Noah and me. In my dazed state, I wondered if that had actually happened or if I had dreamt it. As I contemplated what was real, the fog in my brain lifted, and I realized I was in the hospital. An orange glow came from a small, single window in the room, indicating the sun was close to the horizon.

I turned my head to see Noah asleep in a recliner. He was in gray sweatpants and a black T-shirt. His hair was a mess, and he needed to shave. His frown made me wonder if he had slept much. It was different from the serene expression I had witnessed when I previously woke up next to him.

I found the call button and pressed it, hoping not to wake him. Moments later, a male nurse entered the room. With shaky hands,

I lifted one finger to my lips and pointed to Noah. The nurse moved close and leaned over.

"It's nice to see you awake," the middle-aged slender man said with a kind voice.

"Thank you," I said, raspy and hoarse. "I'm sorry to bother you, but I'm really thirsty."

This was an understatement. My throat felt like I had swallowed a desert.

"I'll get you some water."

The nurse was one foot out of the door when Noah clasped my hand. I turned my head back to him.

"I could have done that. You should have woken me up."

"You looked like you needed the sleep." My voice cracked from my dry throat. "Noah, exactly what happened? Did Vlad really try to shoot you?"

"Paige, babe." It was only then I noticed the dark circles under his eyes, and that they were bloodshot and full of tears. "What were you thinking? I did everything I could to protect you, and you—you stepped in front of a bullet. Two bullets, actually. How in the hell am I supposed to keep you safe if you are going to do insane things like that?"

"I wasn't going to let Vlad hurt you. I wasn't going to let him win."

"You almost died." His voice cracked. "You nearly bled out in the ambulance. And then things just went from bad to worse during the surgery. You were in the operating room for hours. We weren't sure if you were going to wake up."

Looking into his emotion-filled eyes, I knew he needed reassurance, so I grasped his hand that was resting on the bed.

"But I didn't die. I'll be fine. I just need some time to heal."

I stopped talking when the nurse returned with a sealed bottle of water and handed it to Noah. Noah examined the bottle carefully before opening it. Once it was open, he held it to my lips, and I took a few small sips.

"The doctor will be doing his morning rounds in about an hour. He'll be glad to see you awake."

"We all are," Noah said.

"So, it's Tuesday?" I asked.

The two men glanced at one another.

Noah nodded, and the nurse left. "No, beautiful. It's Friday morning."

I had lost a week. It took time for me to come to terms with the concept. I was too exhausted to talk but Noah understood and sat beside me. He turned the television on and shot a text to someone.

The longer I remained awake, the more relaxed Noah appeared. His relief at my improved health was apparent.

I looked around, only then seeing the overflowing flower arrangements, a multitude of balloons, and a few stuffed animals. However, only one made me smile. In a clear glass sat my wedding bouquet. I last remembered holding it when Noah kissed me outside of the courthouse.

As the morning news shows began, Phoebe arrived with breakfast for Noah and me, freshly made from Thomas Hall. The omelet, toast, and melon looked delicious, but I was too weak to eat them without assistance. I watched Noah inhale his breakfast and wondered when he'd last eaten.

Phoebe sat on the edge of the bed. Love and respect radiated from her towards me in a way it hadn't before. Taking a bullet for her son had erased any doubts of our union she may have had.

"Need help?" she whispered in a sweet, mothering tone.

I nodded, and she cut up the omelet, feeding me small mouthfuls as she went. The eggs were fluffy and a little sweet. The peppers, onions, ham, along with gooey cheddar cheese, created the perfect balance.

As soon as Noah was done, he took his sweet mother's place. I couldn't finish it all and told Noah to help himself to the rest after I'd eaten a little more.

I was struggling to stay awake when Noah and Phoebe began to argue about Noah going home to shower and sleep. It was only when I spoke up that Noah listened.

"You should go home. Mom said she'd stay with me, and I'm going to fall asleep soon anyway."

I wasn't sure what Phoebe would think of me calling her mom but one look at her smile told me all I needed to know.

"Now I understand what Uncle Edward meant when he said he didn't like it when Aunt Cassie and Gran ganged up on him." He turned his attention solely to me. "I'll go home once you're asleep, but I won't stay gone long. I'll bring lunch and dinner for us when I come back."

"I can just eat the tray they bring to the room."

Phoebe and Noah looked at each other.

"No, dear, you can't. Someone tried to poison your food the first night you were in this room," Phoebe explained.

"What?!"

"Tuesday afternoon, the doctor moved you from intensive care to this room. At dinnertime, a small blonde nurse I'd never seen before and haven't seen since brought in a tray." Noah said. "She said it was an extra one, and she thought I might be hungry. I only ate a few bites because it tasted weird. An hour later, I was in the emergency room being treated because, when the food was tested, it was laced with cyanide. I really only got my appetite back today."

I muttered, "His game's not over. Not yet."

My world began to close in on me.

But I don't think anyone heard me because Phoebe continued where Noah left off without commenting. "That's why there are guards outside your door. The list of visitors allowed in is small, and all of your food is coming from Thomas Hall."

I was overwhelmed and began to shake.

"We're going to die, aren't we? He's going to kill us both."

Before I could finish my question, Noah had me in his arms.

"We don't know who tried to poison you. Vlad's in jail."

"It's got to be Alexei, my stepfather. And it wasn't meant for me. It was meant for you!" It wasn't until that moment that I realized that Vlad wasn't in Willow Creek alone. "I've got to go! Go far away! He's going to kill you if I stay!"

I pulled away from Noah, and when I sat up, I felt the burning from the stitches in my abdomen pulling against my skin. Once upright, I hung my unsteady, clumsy legs over the side of the bed and attempted to stand. Noah had to fight against me walking and then wrapped me in his arms to put me back into bed.

"No, I'm not going to die, and neither are you. You're just overwhelmed. You don't even know for sure that he is here."

I wasn't certain if Noah was trying to calm me or reassure himself because the panic about what he had gotten into by marrying me was written all over his face.

I didn't see him press the morphine drip button, but he must have. Because, moments later, I drifted off into a dreamless sleep.

The next day, I dozed off just after lunch, with Noah sitting beside me and holding my hand. When I woke three hours later, Faith was sitting in the recliner, reading a book.

"Hey, friend," I said.

She smiled, closed her book, and focused her attention on me. "Hey. Did you have a good rest?"

"Yeah. Where's Noah?"

"I sent him home for a bit. He claimed he was fine but looked exhausted."

"Thanks. I've had mixed results getting him to go home and sleep."

"Somedays are easier than others."

"Wait?" I paused, confused. "You've done this before?"

"Every day. You've just slept through it until today."

I couldn't ask for a better friend. And now, she was family, too.

"Faith, I love you."

"I love you, too, Paige."

She walked over to the bed and wrapped me in a hug. We held each other for a few seconds before I heard the sound of my husband's voice.

"Hello, ladies."

Both Faith and I turned our heads towards the door. He walked to me and planted a kiss on my forehead after Faith released me. He sat on the edge of the bed and played with my hair as I leaned into him.

"I just saw your doctor in the hall," Noah said. "He says if you continue improving, he'll discharge you at the beginning of the week."

I smiled. I was ready to go home.

Chapter Fifteen

IT WAS LATE MONDAY afternoon when I was finally released from the hospital, and we were able to make it to the front door of our house at Thomas Hall. That morning, the doctor removed what seemed like hundreds of stitches from my surgery but stressed the importance of a month's rest for the remaining internal stitches to dissolve.

My spleen had taken the bulk of the damage, and a bullet had grazed my pancreas. The surgery had ended with a splenectomy. Without a spleen, I would be at higher risk of infection for the rest of my life. The doctors seemed hopeful that my pancreas would continue to work properly but sent me home with a blood glucose monitor to check my blood sugar daily for the next month until I returned for a follow-up appointment.

Noah had a tight grip on my waist, keeping me stable as I slowly walked from the limo to the door. Just as we reached the threshold, he scooped me up, and I wrapped my arms around his neck.

He carried me into the house like a groom would traditionally carry his bride over the threshold. I expected him to put me down, but he didn't. Instead, he softly pressed his lips against mine. "Where do you want to go? The sofa? The bed?"

"The sofa, I think. I'm sick of being in a bed."

He carried me to the den and placed me on the sofa, grunting as he did. He was still rolling his shoulder when he turned on sixties music from the app on his phone and sat beside me.

"Why don't I call up to Gran's and have dinner sent down?"

"I wish I was well enough to cook for you."

"You like to cook?"

"Sometimes. I prefer to bake. What about you?"

"I like to cook with other people. Being in the kitchen alone is no fun."

"We should do that. Once I'm a little stronger."

Noah kissed me again. After, I leaned against him and closed my eyes. I was more tired than I thought. The next time I opened my eyes, the moonlight was pouring through the windows as the aroma of curry swirled around the room, and I could hear Noah talking to Cassandra and Colin somewhere in the house.

I slowly stood, careful not to lose my balance, and made my way down the hall. There, I found the three in the kitchen, sitting on the stools at the island, drinking wine.

"Hey, what are you doing up?" Noah asked as he rushed to help me to a stool.

"I didn't mean to fall asleep."

"It's okay."

"Are you hungry?" Colin asked, his Irish accent heavy.

I loved working with him at the brewery. He was such a big teddy bear, always sweet and kind.

"A little."

Without saying a word, Cassandra scurried around the kitchen and within minutes, then placed a hot bowl of butter chicken and jasmine rice with peas in front of me.

After I took my first bite, I looked at them, all carefully watching my every move. "What were y'all talking about before I interrupted you?"

"Violet," Cassandra said.

I focused my attention on Colin. "Is she working out okay at the brewery?"

"Yes. It's a busier pace than the winery, and it took her a few days to find her way around, but she's doin' fine. We were talkin' about her and Sam."

"Her and Sam?"

"Sam's had a crush on her since they were kids," Noah said.

"Oh. I didn't know that." I ate a few more bites of my dinner, but was full long before the bowl was empty.

Once I was done, my eyelids were heavy. I saw Colin nudge Cassandra gently between blinks.

"Noah, why don't you help your wife to bed? We'll put the leftovers in the fridge for you before we head out," he said.

As soon as I stood, Cassandra and Colin gave me gentle hugs before Noah carried me up the stairs to our bedroom.

It was a luxurious suite, approximately six hundred square feet, designed for ultimate comfort. The California king-sized mattress rested on a beautifully carved cherry wood frame with matching head and footboards. In addition to a sitting area, there were end tables, lamps, large mirrors, and massive dressers. The walk-in closets were bigger than my room when I was growing up.

He gently sat me on the bed. "What can I do to help you?"

"There's a nightgown in the drawer," I said, pointing to the dresser.

He grabbed it for me. While he did, I tried to pull my shirt over my head. A sharp pain caused me to moan.

"Stop. Let me help."

I obeyed, and he carefully assisted me out of my top. "That's not the way I want you moaning in my bed." He flashed me a mischievous grin. "We'll explore better ways to make you do that once you're completely healed and up for it."

A small laugh escaped the smile on my face, and I felt the pull of where my stitches had been.

"Ouch. Don't make me laugh. Please."

He leaned in for a quick kiss and helped strip clothes off of me until I was wearing nothing but my bra and panties.

"Now, should I continue helping, or do you want to finish with me somewhere else?"

"I don't think I can undo the bra myself, so you should probably stay. Plus, I heard you tell Gran you peeked at me when I was in the shower the morning of our wedding. I think you've seen it all already."

He grinned sheepishly as he undid the clasps. Bra in hand, he took a long, lingering look at my breasts.

"Damn, I'm a lucky man," he said, raising his eyebrows.

After taking another moment to admire my body, Noah helped me into the short satin nightie Zoe had brought me for our wedding night. He gently brushed and braided my hair before putting me under the covers.

He kissed me on the forehead and said, "I'll be right back. I'm going to make sure the house is locked up."

I was asleep before he returned.

On Tuesday, while having a late lunch and watching *Some Like It Hot*, Noah's phone rang. He fished it from his pocket and showed it to me before answering.

It was Chief Hayes.

"Hey, Brian. What's up?"

"Is Paige with you? If so, put me on speaker. It will save me a call."

"You already are."

"Hello, sir," I said.

"Hi, Paige. I need to let y'all know that it looks like Vlad is about to make bail. Some guy just walked into the station with a wad of cash. The desk officer called me at home to let me know."

As he spoke, nausea rose in my throat, and an icy sweat formed on my brow.

"Brian, can I call you back? Paige isn't looking so good."

"Sure. You've got my number."

By the time the guys hung up, I was on my feet. Wanting to run.

There was only one person who could and would bail him out. His father, Alexei.

Before I could take a single step, Noah scooped me into his arms. "Look at me." When I followed his command, he continued. "It's going to be okay."

"No. Alexei is here."

"You really think he's in Willow Creek?"

"Who else would it be?"

"I wouldn't be so sure. It was probably a bail bondsman. People hire them all the time."

"I think you are underestimating how relentless Alexei is."

The exasperation I felt of Noah's misguided confidence in the Orlov family giving up on me was unmeasurable. He was overly confident of my safety at Thomas Hall as well, causing me to let out a frustrated sigh.

He cradled me gently and carried me up to bed. "You need to rest," he said, then fetched me a cool washcloth and a glass of water.

I dozed off moments later, exhausted from the emotional duress but knowing, deep in my soul, that Alexei Orlov was in town.

And he was coming to get me.

·❤·❤·❤·❤·❤·

It had only taken me seconds to fall asleep, but when I opened my eyes, the bedside clock read eleven seventeen, classical music softly filled the room, and I was alone. I changed into one of Noah's T-shirts, slipped on his robe and searched the dark house. Noah wasn't there. I grabbed a bottle of water and took it back to bed with me. Knowing I wouldn't be able to go back to sleep immediately, I lay in bed and read one of the many books Cassandra brought over the night I came home from the hospital. Even though I wasn't familiar with Charlaine Harris, I was enjoying the alternate universe fiction with a strong female main character.

Just after midnight, I dozed off with the book in my lap and the bedside lamp on. The next thing I knew, I was waking to daylight pouring through the windows, Noah's cell phone ringing, and my husband stirring next to me from the sound.

He answered his phone and put it on speaker. "Yes?"

"Noah, it's Brian Hayes."

"Oh. Hey. Good morning."

"I'm calling because Vladimir Orlov was found dead in a dumpster behind the motel in town this morning."

I gasped. Shocked by my own reaction, I jumped from the bed and walked across the room to the window.

"Was that Paige I just heard?"

"Yeah," Noah answered. "We slept in this morning."

"The medical examiner says he was murdered sometime between midnight and two this morning. I hate to ask, but I have to since you are both suspects. Where were the two of you at this time?"

Before Noah could say a word, I spoke up.

"We were here, asleep. Well, mostly asleep. I woke up a little before one o'clock this morning and got a glass of water."

"And Noah was with you?"

I locked eyes with Noah.

"Yes, he was. He was snoring."

"Okay. I might need that in writing. I'll let you know if I do."

Once we were off the phone with Chief Hayes, I sat on the edge of the bed and Noah joined me.

"Why?" he asked.

"Because you needed an alibi, and going for a drive alone at midnight isn't a good one."

"Paige, I—"

"Stop. I don't want to know. You're alibied, and that is all that's important."

"I'll talk to you soon," Noah said, hitting the end button to finish the call.

Earlier that day, we discovered that both the Washington DC and Richmond newspapers had learned we were married and Noah's friends had been phoning ever since. I didn't realize Noah knew so many people, and I had kept my post-New Orleans life confined. The fewer people I knew, the less chance of word getting to Ferma of my whereabouts, having learned that lesson the hard way in Louisiana.

"My phone has been ringing off the hook all day, but yours hasn't. Why is that?"

"Noah, you have a big social life. I'm just beginning to understand that. You know, just because you married me doesn't mean that has to stop. If you want to go out at night, I don't mind. I can find something here to do."

He slowly worked his way across the room, reminding me of a tiger stalking its prey. When he reached me, he pounced, wrapping his arms around me and lifting me until we were face-to-face. What followed was a warm, passionate kiss.

"No, I don't want to go anywhere without you. Hell, I hate the idea of leaving for work in the morning. You and this marriage are my primary focus now. Nothing else matters."

He carefully lowered me to the floor. He would never admit it, but I could tell his shoulder was causing him pain.

"But you've been restless. I can tell. Wanting to do things in the evenings. You're sick of reading and watching basketball on TV at night. You've been a good sport about it but—"

"But nothing." He paused and seemed to have a light bulb moment. "Of course you don't get it. You don't know."

"Know what?" I asked.

He pulled me close and gently held me. "Married people do married things."

"What do you mean *married things*?"

"You know, couples stuff. Go on dinner dates. See a movie. Play tennis. Do you play tennis?"

"No, but I've always wanted to learn."

"We can make that happen. There's a court here, at Thomas Hall. My father was a tennis pro. Mom had it built in an effort to make him happy."

"It didn't work?" I asked, already knowing the answer.

Noah's phone rang again. If we were talking, he'd normally ignore it. However, he was trying to avoid responding to my question, so he answered it but put it on speaker. He rarely spoke of his father unless it was absolutely imperative to the conversation.

"Dude, you got married? What the fuck?" a man with a deep bass voice said through the speaker.

"You're on speaker, Larry. And don't swear around my wife."

"Sorry, ma'am."

"Please, don't *ma'am* me. It's nice to meet you, Larry. I'll let you two catch up. I'm going to go pour myself some iced tea." I turned to Noah. "Want any?"

He nodded, and I headed to the kitchen, where I could still hear everything. As I filled glasses with ice, they continued their conversation.

"I used Hope's wedding to finally make my move on Paige, and it worked. We got married ten days later."

"Wait? Is she the tiny blonde you were dancing with that night?"

"Yep."

"Damn, you are one lucky guy. But why the rush?"

I waited for the long-winded explanation to come but was surprised by Noah's response.

"Neither of us wanted anything high profile. We just wanted to start our lives together. So, we went to City Hall and made it happen."

While our marriage had become common knowledge, apparently, the shooting hadn't. While I was in the hospital, Cassandra went to the local newspaper's office and explained that my life was still in danger and running the article could expose my location.

To avoid an article on the shooting, Cassandra agreed to an interview on life at Thomas Hall and made a sizable donation to the community college's English department, where the paper's editor taught.

"Wow! Does this mean no more parties or hanging out?"

"Right now, it's all about my wife."

He said this as I walked into the room with his drink.

"So, throw a party for her."

I enjoyed the occasional party, so I added my two cents.

"That's not a bad idea. You can invite all your friends, and we can celebrate getting married."

"Really?" Noah liked the idea of something social. He would never admit it, but he'd been craving it.

"Yeah. Throwing parties can be a married thing, right?"

Noah smiled, and his bright eyes sparkled with excitement.

"You should do it at the Congressional Country Club. I can arrange it. My family has a membership."

"It needs to be at Thomas Hall," Noah said. "Crazy ex, so there are security issues."

"Which one of your ex-girlfriends did you piss off?"

"Not mine, one of Paige's exes."

And while that wasn't the whole truth, it was an easy answer.

Chapter Sixteen

"I NEED TO GO into town tomorrow and pick up a few things," I said as we finished our dinner.

"But you're safe here."

I knew this would be Noah's response. He was growing single-minded with his protectiveness. His mantra had become that I was safe as long as I was at Thomas Hall.

"Vlad is dead. I'm safe now."

I really didn't believe it, but it was time for me to get back to my life. Having spent over a dozen years looking over my shoulder, I knew I'd probably have to do so for the remainder of my life.

"Still, you're safer here."

"I need some clothes. Even with the clothes Faith gave me and the couple of outfits Zoe brought by the house, I am still in need of some things."

"You don't need to leave Thomas Hall for that. Tell me what you need, and I'll have them picked up."

"I'd prefer to pick out my own bras and panties."

Noah stood, only to drop to his knees once he reached me on the other side of the table.

"I can do that for you," he said with a wicked smile as his arms wrapped around me, and his hands found their way under my shirt and onto bare skin. "But I'd rather be responsible for the removal of them than the purchase."

I shook my head and laughed. "I'm beginning to think you have a one-track mind."

"Can you blame me? I have a beautiful wife." He wiggled his eyebrows up and down, making me laugh even more.

"So, I think you should take your wife shopping soon," I said in a teasing tone.

"Okay. I'll make arrangements for a trip into Willow Creek tomorrow."

The next morning, after breakfast, I assumed Noah would go to work. Instead, he called Faith to let her know he would be late.

When we stepped out the door to leave, we were met by a stretch limo, a driver, and two bodyguards. I hesitated when we reached the car until I felt Noah's hand on the small of my back.

"We can cancel this if you've changed your mind."

He wanted me to stay put, and this was his polite way of making me think it was my idea not to go.

I suddenly didn't feel as brave as I had when I made the suggestion the night before. I took a deep breath before pushing the fear from my mind.

"I've got to leave Thomas Hall at some point."

We didn't talk on the way into town. Noah held me, and I snuggled in as close as I could. He always smelled of sweet wine and vanilla, and I found it intoxicating.

When we pulled up to Zoe's shop, the parking spot in front of the store had been blocked off for us. The security guards got out first, moved the cones, and the driver parked. All of the security measures Noah had insisted left me feeling conspicuous.

"I thought we were going with the 'keep a low profile' approach."

"We are going with the 'keep my wife alive' approach. Got a problem with that, Mrs. Foster?"

He had never called me Mrs. Foster before, and I giggled, causing a broad smile from him.

We were hurried into Zoe's boutique, where she immediately locked the door and hung a closed for lunch sign.

"How are my favorite newlyweds?" Zoe asked as she gave us hugs. "Don't tell Hope and Grayson I said that."

"We are great," Noah announced. "But as you know, Paige needs clothes."

"I can live with what I have clothing-wise, but I need underwear, bras, and nightgowns."

Noah pulled out his phone. "I made a list last night after you fell asleep. You have two dresses, one pair of heels, one pair of flats, two pairs of pants, four shirts, a satin robe, and one nightgown. My wife needs clothes."

"Good god," Zoe exclaimed. "I pack more than that for an overnight trip. Let's get busy."

"Wait," I said, turning to Noah. "I can't afford this. Two bra and underwear sets are going to drain my bank account. I haven't been able to work, remember?"

"Babe, I've got this. You don't have to worry about money ever again."

"Noah, that's not why I married you."

"I know, but this will make me happy. Remember when we first started dating and I said I would take care of you? Well, this is part of that. Husbands buy their wives beautiful things." He glanced at Zoe and smiled. "This is the part where she whispers my name. I love when she does that." Then he leaned in from behind me and quietly said, "It's the sexiest thing I've ever heard in my life."

When I turned, I found myself in his arms. I didn't know whether to smack his arm for calling me out or whisper his name, so I did neither. Instead, I stood on my toes and kissed him. He moved one hand from my waist to the nape of my neck and deepened the kiss. I forgot where we were until Zoe spoke up.

"Okay, you two, save that for home. Let's build you a wardrobe."

An hour and a half later, multiple bags were being loaded into the trunk of the limo and Noah was at the register settling the bill with Zoe. I was sitting in a chair, exhausted, looking out the window onto Main Street.

And that's when I saw my stepfather. He was walking down the sidewalk, heading in the direction of Zoe's shop.

Alexei looked the same as he had the last time I saw him so many years ago. His hair was still silver, long, and pulled into a low ponytail. He was wearing jeans and a button-down collared shirt.

I knew in my gut who had killed Vlad, and it wasn't my husband. My stepfather was brutal when punishing people, and I was certain he felt Vlad's death was justified. He had provided no children to the Orlov family while I was at Ferma and had failed to retrieve me. If Alexei had come all the way from California, he had no intention of leaving without me.

I was panicked and wanted to run.

As I stood, Noah was walking toward me. He must have seen the terror in my expression.

"Paige, what is it?"

"He's here. In Willow Creek." I pointed out the window before hiding behind Noah.

"He looks like an older version of Vlad," Noah said, and Zoe joined us, expanding the human wall blocking me from the window.

"It's my stepfather, Alexei. I told you he was here. I should have trusted myself and stayed at Thomas Hall. But you were so sure, and I wanted to believe you. I just want my life back."

I tried to escape, racing for the back door. However, Noah wrapped me in his arms to keep me from fleeing. He said nothing, but in less than a minute, we were in the limo and heading back to Thomas Hall. Once outside the town, I looked at Noah, who was singularly focused on me.

"No more leaving Thomas Hall for a while," I said.

"No running away, either," he interjected. "You are safe at Thomas Hall."

He was convinced the place was a fortress, but I knew that no plan was perfect, and that Alexei, with his relentless nature, would find a way.

"Are you sure you're up for this?" Noah asked as I stepped into my heels.

I don't know how, but a member of Vivian's staff had gotten the blood splatter off the toe of one of them. It was a good thing, too. At the moment, the white Louboutin heels were the only dress shoes I owned besides the black leather strappy heels Noah bought me at Zoe's shop.

"I'm not running a marathon. It's Sunday dinner."

"Dinner at Gran's can feel like running a marathon. If it gets to be too much, let me know."

I turned to Noah. "Do I look okay?"

I was wearing a dress Faith had given me. She and I were about the same size. During my hospital stay, she brought over some of her rarely worn clothes for me to wear when I got home. It seemed to be an appropriate Sunday dinner dress. It was royal blue, with a full skirt and white pearl buttons, giving it a retro fifties vibe.

Noah hooked my waist with one arm and wrapped the other around my neck.

"You look spectacular. But you always do. You always have."

The last word was barely out of his mouth before his lips were on mine. Man, did my husband know how to kiss. His mouth on mine would make my head spin when I wasn't recovering from a gunshot wound. It was no surprise that, when it ended, I swayed. He steadied me with a worrisome smile.

"You're going to have to be careful kissing me like that. I may never be steady on my feet again."

"Then, I guess I'll just have to hold you forever." He smiled as he kept me close to his side.

I was the luckiest girl in the world.

"We should go," I said, and Noah guided me to the front door.

A golf cart was waiting for us, so I wouldn't have to walk.

I hesitated before stepping outside, and he read my thoughts.

"You're safe here. Alexei can't reach you here."

Noah had said these words so many times that they were beginning to sound meaningless. I just hoped Thomas Hall was the fortress everyone now claimed it to be and that what he was saying was true.

Noah and I had barely arrived at the main house when Miss Vivian pulled me into the sunroom.

"I have something for you." She made her way to a small writing table, opened a drawer, and retrieved a weathered, handmade patchwork pouch. She handed it to me before saying anything more.

"These belonged to my Great Aunt Clara. She was very talented with tarot cards. Me, not so much."

Strong, positive vibes radiated from the pouch. They were familiar and warm and felt more right in my hands than my recently destroyed set. It was as though they were meant to be mine.

I opened it and slid the antique cards out. They were probably made in the mid-to-late 1800s and were gorgeously illustrated with gold foil edges. Some of the foil had worn off over the century they had existed, but even in their current state, they were a much more detailed set than I previously owned. Each card was hand-illustrated with classic but still vibrant colors. I took a long moment to look at each card.

I was pleasantly surprised to discover that Miss Vivian's background included more than your typical Southern Christian teachings. While I believed in the Bible and Christ, I believed there was more and, so it seemed, Vivian did as well.

"These are fantastic! But are you sure you want to part with them?"

"They've sat in a box for the last sixty years. They deserve to be used."

"They have a lot of energy. I'll need to get some candles and incense to use them properly. Some salt and sage, too."

"I'll have a member of the staff get them for you and bring everything over this evening."

Before we returned to the library, where the others waited, Miss Vivian had made arrangements for the staff to deliver it all, along with the cards as well.

We left the main house around eight o'clock. The rest of the family was still there, but I was starting to doze off in one of the overstuffed chairs in the library. Noah announced to everyone that I needed to rest, and we said our good nights. As soon as he settled me into the passenger seat of the golf cart, his face turned red and angry.

"You were supposed to tell me if you got tired. Why didn't you?"

He was right. I was exhausted. I was ready to call it a night when the main course was served.

"I know. But I was enjoying your family so much. And I didn't want to miss a thing. I can't believe Gran had a new wedding cake made for us to have tonight."

"Still, you need your rest."

"Noah, I don't think you understand." Pools of tears filled my eyes. "I never had this. Family who truly cared for each other is not something I ever remember. I think it was there with my father, but he died when I was seven. I don't have too many memories of life before his death."

Noah's expression quickly changed from anger to understanding. He leaned over and kissed my forehead. "I'm sorry. I didn't mean to get angry. I just want you healthy. Sometimes, I forget your body isn't the only thing that needs healing. It sounds like my family might be what your heart needs to heal, too."

As soon as we entered the front door, I slipped off my shoes and rubbed my sore feet. I had worn heels more in the last month than I had in my entire life, and my feet were feeling the torture.

"Hey, babe. There's a package on the coffee table for you."

I walked into the den to find a gorgeous mahogany box with the Tree of Life hand-carved into its lid. I sat next to Noah before I opened it. Inside was everything I needed, along with Great Aunt Clara's tarot cards and a note from Vivian.

> *Paige,*
> *I want a reading soon!*
> *Love,*
> *Gran*

I smiled.

Miss Vivian was really the most wonderful person I ever met. And now she was my grandmother. My family.

"Who is it from?" Noah asked, pulling me away from my thoughts.

I handed him the note, and he smiled.

"She's going to want to know when she's getting great-grandchildren from any of us grandkids," Noah said.

He placed his fingers on my cheek and used his other arm to pull me close. "My guess is yes. And it will be us."

Chaper Seventeen

WHEN I HEARD THE front door close, I was pulling the last of the teacakes from the oven. After doing nothing for so long, the need to do something productive was overwhelming. I loved baking and found it relaxing. The measuring, mixing, and aroma of the cookies in the oven were like meditation for me, and it left me feeling more relaxed than I had been since Hope's wedding.

"Hey, babe. I'm home," Noah said as he walked toward the kitchen. He froze when he reached the doorway.

I watched as he stared at the counter and the cookies I baked throughout the afternoon. I expected him to be at least cheerful to find a house filled with chocolate chip, peanut butter, and teacake cookies.

"What the hell are you doing? We talked about this last night. You're supposed to be resting."

"Rest is boring. I couldn't stand to lie around, doing nothing any longer."

He took the spatula from my hands as he spoke. "Living room. Now."

His attitude cemented my feet to the floor. I crossed my arms, glaring at him. "Excuse me? What did you just say?"

"You heard me. I said into the living room."

If I moved or said a word, I would lose my temper.

When I didn't respond, he stomped over to me, and I stared him down. As I did, I became lightheaded and nauseous. My mind raced back to the first time I had attempted defiance after arriving at Ferma and the violence that followed.

Noah scooped me up with the intent of carrying me into the den to deposit me on the sofa. When he did, I was snapped back to my reality. Before he could get far, I pounded on his chest with my fists.

"Put me down!" I screamed into his ear.

"No! You need to rest. I have to take care of you."

"Stop it! I can't do this anymore. You don't want to take care of me. You just want to control me!"

Noah froze, his eyes growing large, and he carefully slid me down him until my feet were on the floor in the hallway. As soon as he did, he rolled his sore shoulder.

"Why would you say that?" he asked slowly and calmer than he'd been just moments earlier.

"Why? Why! You have me trapped here. I sit here all day, listening to music and reading books. I am bored out of my mind! And I can't leave."

"It's just until we know you're safe."

"No! I can't leave! I have no car! Even if I did, I couldn't put gas in it. I have no money! Why? Because I can't work right now. I have nothing! I'm trapped!"

"That's what this is really about? Control?" He pulled his wallet from the back pocket, handing me the entire thing. Then he grabbed his keys from a hook by the door and dropped them on the table next to us. "Take whichever car you want. Both sets are on that ring."

"I don't want any of this from you," I said, throwing his wallet at him and hitting his jaw. "I can't! I can't live like this anymore!"

I ran from the house, only pausing to grab my shoes at the door. Whether Noah would follow me, I didn't care. After stopping to pant and catch my breath, I slipped my tennis shoes on and walked. Wanted to head toward the gate and escape this gilded cage. But there was no point. I had nothing. No way to survive beyond the gates surrounding Thomas Hall.

I walked until I reached the main house and continued left on the looping path of the grounds. I walked until I passed the pool and pool house on the left and didn't stop until I reached the front door of Cassandra's home.

I rang the bell, and Cassandra answered. One look at me, and she knew.

"First argument?" I nodded, and she invited me into the house, guiding me to the kitchen.

Only when we reached the island did she start asking questions.

"What was the argument about?"

"Cookies."

"Cookies?"

"Well, sort of. He got mad because I was making cookies and not resting."

Then Cassandra gave me *The Look*. I had seen her give it to Hope before but didn't realize how truth-inspiring it could be. Words flowed from me, and it was impossible to stop them.

"I feel trapped. Like I've been held hostage ever since I said, 'I do.' First, by the hospital and the doctors. Now by Noah and Thomas Hall."

It was the first time I had been able to succinctly express my feelings.

"Sounds like there is a lot to unpack here. Sit down, and we'll chat. But first, tea."

Watching her prepare hot tea was almost ceremonial. The way she stirred the loose leaves before scooping the level spoonfuls into a filter basket that fit into the beautiful purple ceramic teapot with a brass handle. She carefully watched the water heat until it was exactly two hundred and twelve degrees. After steeping the tea for precisely three minutes, she poured it into matching mugs and offered milk and sugar, which I declined. Few people had a genuine appreciation for the art of making tea, and it seemed she and I were two of them.

"Okay, talk to me."

"I don't know how he doesn't understand how I feel."

"Did you tell him you were feeling this way before today?"

I stared at the teapot before sheepishly answering.

"No."

"Paige, I understand you feel like you are caged in here. I felt the same way occasionally the first few years I lived here. But you have to remember, for Noah, this is home."

"So? When I was living at Ferma, which was my home, I felt trapped there, too."

"But was that really a loving environment?"

"No." I closed my eyes and shook my head.

Cassandra wanted me to see Noah's side of this, but it wasn't about him. It was about me and the impossible situation I had fallen into. I needed a girl's girl who would automatically side with me, and Cassandra was not that person.

"Paige, what is it you want that you currently don't have?"

Her question surprised me. Was it freedom? Safety? I honestly didn't know, so I ignored the question.

Before Noah and I married, I lived a life of total independence. I didn't need anything from anyone. Since leaving the courthouse, I was utterly dependent on an overprotective, overbearing man. And I hated the lack of control I had over my life.

"I don't know, but is what Noah is giving me a loving environment? 'Don't do this!' 'I won't let you do that!' 'Why won't you listen to me?' I swear if I hear the words 'It's my job to protect you' one more time, he's going to be the one in need of protection!"

"Sounds like Noah has gotten himself into a bit of trouble," a heavily accented voice said.

I turned to find Colin standing behind me, having returned home from work. He smiled as he made his way to Cassandra, gifting her a handful of tulips and a kiss. He excused himself to change out of his work clothes, and Cassandra began arranging the flowersin a heavy crystal vase.

"I guess I should go back to the house," I said after taking my last sip of tea.

"You know," Cassandra said. "Noah is only behaving this way because he's trying to protect you. Edward was the same way whenever I was in danger."

"I don't care why! Noah is completely insufferable!"

As I stood, Cassandra looked me in the eyes and asked, "Paige, do you know how you sound?"

"Yes, I know. I sound like a brat. A spoiled rotten, selfish brat."

It was true, but admitting it didn't make me feel better. I hated the way I felt and burst into tears.

She walked around the kitchen island and wrapped me in her arms. It was apparent to her I was fighting an internal battle triggered by the argument Noah and I had. I was in so deep that I had no idea how to save myself.

Cassandra guided me to a sitting area just off the kitchen. We sat on the sofa, and she held me while I let all of my frustrations pour out of me with my tears.

As Cassandra released me, there was a knock on the door. We both knew who it was, and Noah didn't wait for anyone to answer but let himself in.

I didn't want to face him, let alone talk to him.

He said nothing but walked straight to me, pulling me from my seat and engulfing me in an embrace. When I tried to pull away, he held me tighter and whispered in my ear.

"I'm sorry. You are right. I don't understand. But I want to."

This time, when I pulled away, he let me. I turned to face Cassandra and saw Colin enter the room, freshly showered in clean clothes. If there was one thing I understood about working at the brewery, it was at the end of the day, you always felt sticky, as if someone had spilled beer on you. When I worked there, I found myself showering every evening as soon as I got home from work.

"Thank you for having me here this afternoon," I said.

Cassandra gave me a sad smile and nodded. "Paige, you don't have to leave right now. You are welcome to stay."

"Thanks, but I should get home. I need to pack up the cookies I made and tidy up the kitchen."

Colin grinned. "Did you say cookies?" He turned to Cassandra. "Paige makes the best cookies ever!"

"I'll send some over," I said, smiling for the first time since I arrived at their home.

I hugged Cassandra and Colin before walking past Noah, not acknowledging his presence as I headed out the door.

Just after crossing the gravel road, the walking path alongside the pool that cut across the grassy field to our house came into view as Noah caught up to me. He took my hand in his and squeezed it.

I did not return the gesture.

Neither of us spoke, and when we reached the house, I went to the kitchen to clean a room I had left in shambles. What I found was a room so spotless that it looked as if the house was about to be put on the market at an open house. The dishes were in the dishwasher, which was running, and the sinks were freshly scrubbed. The countertops sparkled from the sunlight through the pristine glass of the windows, and the floors were spotless.

On the island, dinner awaited us, plated and wrapped in foil. Next to it, the cookies were boxed and stacked as though they came from a bakery, each one an assortment of the freshly baked sweets.

I threw my arms up in exasperation, needing to occupy myself, and the staff left me with nothing to do.

I handed one of the boxes to Noah. "Go take these to Colin."

It was rare for me to bark orders, but he knew better than to argue with me.

While he was gone, I fixed myself a fresh cup of chai, grabbed two cookies, and headed to our bedroom. After eating the cookies, I curled up on the bed, too frustrated to do anything else. I hated feeling this trapped. My decisions of the last few weeks were smothering me.

When he returned, I heard Noah close the door. He never shut a door quietly. When he called out for me, I said nothing. Moments later, he raced up the stairs, exhaling when he reached our door and saw me lying on the bed.

"Thank God. I thought you left."

"Can't. Nowhere for me to go. No way to get there."

Tears streamed down my face.

He climbed onto the bed, spooning with me. Neither of us spoke. We just stayed there, listening to the music I had put on that morning until I fell asleep.

Chaper Eighteen

WHEN I OPENED MY eyes, the room was no longer bright, as the sun had dropped just below the horizon. The window revealed pink skies that would soon be inky and full of stars. Noah's body was still spooned against mine, but he was talking on the phone with his mother. He had the speaker on, but the volume was turned low.

"Show her some grace, son." Phoebe's voice was calm and sweet. "She has been through so much. It sounds like she bottled her feelings up for many years. You should be happy she feels safe and secure enough to express herself openly to you."

"I know. Catching a wallet to the face was not fun, though."

Phoebe laughed, causing me to chuckle.

"Mom, I've got to go. Sleeping Beauty is laughing at me."

I twisted in his arms so we were face-to-face.

Noah was smiling. "Hey, beautiful."

"Hey. I'm sorry I threw your wallet at you."

"It's okay. It could have been worse. Could have been the keys."

I nodded once.

"Feeling better?"

"I don't know."

"Well, maybe this will help." He handed me a box wrapped with a simple bow.

Opening the box, I discovered a beautiful embossed rainbow-colored leather ostrich skin Brahmin wallet.

"It's beautiful."

"Look inside."

I undid the closure, not expecting to find a credit card, debit card, insurance card, and cash inside. I tried to hand it back to him.

"I've already told you. I don't want this. No matter how pretty you wrap it up."

"Why? I know one of the reasons you feel trapped is because you have no money. Now you do."

"But it's your money."

Noah stared at me and tilted his head. He sighed and a moment of realization fell onto his face. "Babe, a marriage is a union, right?"

"Right."

"It's a union of everything. Mind, body, heart, soul, and assets. What's mine is yours. What's yours is mine. So, I want you to take it and just put it away even if you don't want it now. In case you ever need it. In case you want to leave. I don't want you ever to feel caged in like you have tonight. Okay?"

"I can't. I'll know it's your money, not mine."

"I thought you might say that. What about this? Take it, and when you get your trust fund at the end of the year, you can give me the money back."

"I don't know how much I'm going to get. For all I know, it could be ten dollars and a pack of bubble gum."

Noah laughed at my comment, and I smirked.

"If that's all it is, then I will have just purchased the most expensive pack of gum in recorded history."

He gave me a tight squeeze of a hug before I examined the wallet. With the two thousand dollars in cash and an American Express Black card, I could escape far away from Virginia if I so ever wished. It was a hard gift to turn down, so I set it on my nightstand.

"Okay. Thank you." I hesitated. "After tonight, do you want me to leave?"

I knew if the roles were reversed, I would be completely over me.

"What do you even mean by that?" He was trying to hold his emotions in check, but the tiniest bit of frustration bled through. "Of course I want you here. We're married. We aren't going to walk away from this. Not over cookies."

Noah squeezed me tight once more, pulling me back to him.

"But it's not really about cookies, is it?" he asked.

I shook my head.

"I need to be more aware of how you're feeling. This obviously isn't an emotion that just popped up overnight. It had been brewing for a while, hadn't it?"

This sounded logical. Too logical for Noah's state of constant stress. I wondered if Colin had spoken with him when he delivered the cookies.

"I guess." I watched as a vein on his forehead popped to the surface and knew he was about to lose his cool.

"Then, why the fuck didn't you say something sooner?"

His exasperated tone and quick change from caring to edgy told me that his patience was gone. But so was mine, and words flew out of my mouth without consideration.

"Quit swearing at me," I snapped. "Nobody held a gun to your head and forced you to marry me. As a matter of fact, I tried to talk you out of it. I knew, one day, you'd hate me for this. I just thought it would take a little longer!"

"Why the hell do you do that?"

"Do what?"

"Try to convince me you're not worth what I have to offer."

"Because I'm not!"

He froze, and the anger he'd been holding in his clenched facial muscles melted away, and the vein on his forehead sank back into his skin, revealing a softness that could only be described as angelic. When he finally spoke, his voice was tender.

"Babe, that is so far from the truth."

While he was calmer, I was still living in a moment of self-hate. My first instinct was to scream, but my response came out raspy and breathless.

"I'm broken," I choked out, then inhaled. "Noah, I know you think we can fix this, but Vlad and Alexei and that whole damn cult broke me. You deserve so much more than I can give you."

"There is nothing broken about you, babe. Life has just beaten you up a little," Noah said as he rested his fingertips on my cheek.

I shook my head, knowing he was wrong.

"Have you always felt this way?"

"What do you mean?"

"For the last four years, I've watched you at work and at parties at Thomas Hall. You are always upbeat and optimistic. Completely confident in everything you do."

"That's work. It's easy to leave everything I hate about myself at home and be the person I wish I could be. But I can't fake it all the time. Eventually, I have to be the person life has turned me into."

"And right now, you can't go to work and escape all that pain you live with."

What he said was a revelation to me. I paused and thought about my feelings throughout the afternoon. "I'm stuck swimming in it, aren't I?"

"Let me be your lifeguard, okay?"

"Weren't you a lifeguard as a teenager?"

"I was. I was good at saving people from drowning. You saved me from a bullet—it's time for me to save you."

·♥·♥·♥·♥·♥·

I crept out of bed with the rising sun, careful not to wake Noah. The night's fitful, sporadic sleep left me wanting answers I couldn't find on my own. When I approached the door, Paco entered the room and gracefully jumped onto the bed. He found my still-warm pillow and positioned himself for a nap. I smiled, thinking about how Noah would react to Paco when he woke.

As I passed through the living room, I grabbed my tarot cards, incense, and matches before making my way to the patio.

It was a beautiful morning. The sunrise created a warm, rosy glow along the horizon, and birdsong filled the air.

After sitting, I cleansed the cards with the sweet-smelling smoke and shuffled the deck. As I did, I felt Vivian's Great Aunt Clara's spirit in the cards. I cut the deck, knocking on it three times before starting to turn each card over.

I rarely read my own cards. Reading other people's cards was much easier than interpreting my own. When I read other people's cards, it was easy to stay impartial. When I read my own, it was easy to interpret them in beneficial ways, but it was not necessarily accurate.

I decided on a Celtic Cross formation with a particular question in mind, but my thoughts were too jumbled to concentrate. It should have been a sign to put the cards away and wait until I was more focused, but I continued with the common ten-card spread anyway.

The first two cards were from the Book of Wands. It wasn't surprising, as I often drew Wands or Swords in my readings and they described my current situation and challenges perfectly. However, I was surprised to see so many major arcana cards appear early on and three in a row. I smiled with The Lovers, which noted my immediate future. The next two cards, the Devil, my root cause card, and Temperance, my aspirations card, bewildered me.

"Maybe the final four cards will help me find the answers I am looking for."

After drawing them, I was pleasantly surprised to see the last card. The Ten of Pentacles. This card represented stability, comfort, and happiness. The tension in my shoulders began to dissipate, knowing that if the cards were right, I would have a happily ever after. I just had to figure out how to get there.

When I did this for a living, I revealed the cards slowly, laying them down one at a time before explaining each card and what it might mean for my client. That morning, though, I had flown through the cards. Realizing my error, I returned to the first card.

I examined the first card carefully. It was the Two of Wands, the crossroads card. I used to tell my customers that it meant they were planning, or getting ready to plan, something life-changing and decisions would have to be made.

"No kidding. Tell me something I don't know," I said out loud, as though Mother Nature herself would hear my plea through the morning air.

The second card felt like more of the same. The Seven of Wands sat in reverse. It wasn't wrong, though. I was emotionally overwhelmed by all the things I was battling at the moment. Most of which were out of my control.

The next card was designed to depict the person's past. From the first time I read my own cards, or even when others read them, the same card always appeared, and this reading was no different. The Eight of Swords. It was a card of great despair and many believed its presence meant an inability to escape your circumstances. For me, it was a constant reminder of my ties to Ferma.

"Will it ever go away? I don't need a reminder of my past."

I heard the sliding glass door open and turned to see my husband with a cup of tea for me and coffee for himself.

"Good morning," he said, kissing the top of my head and placing a cup of tea in front of me. "I was going to join you, but I can see you're busy."

"No, you can stay. I'm just trying to get some perspective on my life." He sat as he looked over the cards. "How did you enjoy waking up next to Paco?"

He laughed. "Next to? He woke me by headbutting me in the face and then batted at my nose with his paws until I got out of bed. Then the furball had the nerve to use my pillow as a bed." As I giggled, he shook his head. "Paco is going to take some getting used to, but he's fun to have around."

"He's been my best friend for years."

"Are the cards helping?"

He was hesitant to ask and even more anxious to know. The previous night had left us both on edge.

"A little," I said, although I'm not sure my response sounded convincing.

"I like that card." He pointed to the next card, my immediate future card. The Lovers.

I smiled. "Me too, but you have to be careful with that one. Remember, things aren't always what they appear to be."

He reached for my left hand and kissed the top of my ring finger where my wedding band rested. After a slight squeeze, he released it. I reached for my cup and sipped the perfectly steeped chai.

"Then what does this one mean?" he asked, tapping The Devil card.

"What do you think it means?" I asked, turning his question back on him.

"I know the first time you read my cards, you said not to take them literally, but I feel like there is something negative about this one."

"You are on the right track. It's my Root Causes card. I would interpret it to mean something had me bound or restricted. Something or someone is holding me in place."

"So, what does it mean when you put it together with all of the cards?" he asked, genuinely interested.

"I'm not sure yet. I wish I had a journal where I could write everything down. Sometimes, returning to it later helps give a fresh perspective."

"I can help with that." Noah stood and returned moments later with a green leather journal.

The name *Foster* was imprinted in gold on the cover. Clipped to it was an onyx fountain pen.

"This is perfect. Thank you. But where did it come from?"

"It was gifted to me ages ago, but I never used it. I knew I needed to save it, but I didn't know why. I guess I was saving it for you."

I placed the journal on the table before climbing into his lap and wrapping my arms around his neck.

"I'm sorry about yesterday," I whispered. "It's all just been so much. Too much. My life has changed so fast. I love being your wife, but everything that's happened around it, well . . ."

"I know, babe. I know. But it will all work out in the end. I promise."

I leaned into him and listened to his heartbeat, silently praying he was right and that we would get to the final card in one piece.

Chapter Nineteen

T HE NEXT DAY, I was debating what to do about lunch. It took three nights, but Noah convinced me I was safe at Thomas Hall. Part of that included Noah staying glued to me at every possible moment, including coming home for lunch daily.

Noah mentioned over breakfast he wouldn't be home for our midday meal due to a dentist appointment but would swing by before returning to his office. As I roamed about the kitchen, the light from the windows disappeared due to the darkening sky. The thunder in the distance grew steadily closer. A fierce storm was on its way.

I flipped on the kitchen light and made myself a peanut butter and jelly sandwich. I hadn't had one since leaving the apartment and my single life behind, where the sandwich had been a staple. As I was about to cut it in half, a crack of thunder and a bolt of lightning simultaneously struck overhead. Seconds later, I was plummeted into darkness.

The sudden silence caused my chest to tighten.

The quiet was eerie. No hum from the refrigerator or music from the Google speaker. The house was insulated well enough to muffle most of the sounds that I thought were rain. It reminded me of Ferma. Parts of it had electricity, but the houses didn't. Since the children at Ferma weren't allowed to play, homes were always noiseless unless the men were talking. Most of the houses didn't even have kitchens. A room where much of a house's sounds are made. We ate breakfast and dinner in the dining hall. No lunch was ever served. As a child, I thought it was because everyone was too busy working. Looking back, it was probably a financial decision.

As the rain poured from the sky, my head hurt from the sinus headache the storm front caused. The longer it lasted, the louder it seemed. My breath became shallow, and I began to shake. I slid down to the floor until I sat with my back against the cabinets. I pulled my knees to my chin, wrapping my body into a tight ball.

I couldn't stop thinking about Ferma—my arrival with my mother, our life's drastic transformation, the children's unkindness, and the adults' captivation with the literate child from Hollywood.

I thought about the beatings, the abuse and the expectations that, by the time I was thirteen, I had learned to accept. At least, that's what I let my mother believe. I spent years lying to her. And why not? She had utterly and thoroughly betrayed me. Multiple times. When I went to her after Vlad raped me the first time and then she watched as Alexei attacked me in the name of teaching

Vlad how to make me submit, I knew there was no hope she would ever be the mother I needed her to be. It devastated me.

Looking back, my mother was never the caregiver when Dad was alive. He was the parent who cared for me. When I started school, I never went home when the day was over. I would be picked up by a limo and delivered to the film studio where Dad made his movies. Most days, I only saw my mother for a few minutes, if at all. Her social appointments kept her far too busy for me.

After Dad died, Mom made a half-hearted effort with me. However, I wondered if I was one of the reasons she agreed to move to Ferma. The children there were raised communally, and she only saw me when she wanted.

My breathing continued to labor as panic set in. I rose to my feet, eager to flee. That was the point I blacked out. Noah would later tell me the rest.

I had a full-blown PTSD episode.

Noah changed his plans when he saw the storm rolling in as he knew I feared both silence and the darkness and didn't want me to be alone. When he arrived, having skipped his appointment, I had my purse and shoes in my hand and was racing toward the door with Paco in the cat carrier.

I knew Noah chose not to tell me everything I had said or done. There was too much time unaccounted for. But I also knew he was trying to spare me the agony of reliving the episode.

"Everyone betrayed me—the Bakers will, too," I said aloud, unaware Noah was in the house. "I've got to get out of here."

"Babe, it's okay. You're okay." Noah tried to wrap me in his arms, but I pushed him away.

"No! I need to go. I'm trapped here. Let me go!"

Tears streamed down my face, and I crumbled into a ball.

The next thing I remembered was waking up on the sofa, with Noah was holding me. I didn't remember him coming in. I only remember being in the kitchen and thinking about my childhood.

I rubbed the sleep from my eyes. "How? Where? When did you get home?"

Noah brushed my hair from my face, pulling the pieces away from my skin that stuck from the tears. He gave me a small, sad smile. "There you are, beautiful. From the looks of it, I got here just in time."

"Just in time?"

"You were going to run away."

"Why would I do that? I mean, I know I've felt trapped lately, but I really do love everything about Thomas Hall. You, your family, the house, the winery, everything."

His smile grew, and some of the sadness faded from his gorgeous brown eyes.

"I'm glad to hear you say that. I don't think you were truly here. I think your mind had taken you somewhere else. You kept saying you were trapped and betrayed. Then you collapsed in my arms and sobbed until you fell asleep."

I began to shake. "Noah, I don't remember leaving the kitchen. Why is this happening to me?"

We both knew the answer to my behavior over the last few days. The arrival of my stepbrother and stepfather had stirred memories of my mother and childhood that I had locked away and had no idea how to manage now that they were free.

We stayed on the sofa, and he continued to hold me, saying nothing. It wasn't long before Paco joined us, jumping onto my lap. After taking some time to settle in, he placed his front paws on Noah's thigh, kneading at it as though he were making biscuits.

When the power was finally restored, Noah sat up, moving me with him.

"Why don't I make us some dinner? Anything you want, at least anything I know how to make."

"Lo mein? It was tasty when you made it last week."

"Sure. Anything you want."

"Don't you need to go back to work for a while first once the storm is over?"

"Paige, it's five-thirty. Everyone is gone for the day and the storm ended a couple of hours ago."

"Wait. What? The power went out at eleven-thirty."

"And I got here around twelve-fifteen."

Something was wrong. This had never happened to me. Seeing these men from my past had turned my world inside out. I lost hours, not minutes, during this terrifying experience and didn't want it to happen again.

My body began to tremble, and he knew I was freaked out.

"It's okay. We'll find someone to help you through this."

I was quiet for the rest of the evening. Dinner was tasty, but Noah still wouldn't let me help. He told me I would need to be cleared by the surgeon before he let me lift a finger.

Chapter Twenty

I WOKE TO FAITH's voice through the speaker of Noah's phone and the morning sun filling our bedroom.

"I know she needs you. She's one of my best friends, and I'm worried about her too, but you've got to come walk the fields with me this morning. I need you. Yesterday's storm included hail that has destroyed everything we can see. We might not have anything to harvest this year." She pleaded with a stressed, cracking voice.

"I understand but Faith, she's—"

"I'll come with him if that's okay." I sat up as I spoke.

Faith and I had become fast friends over the previous six months, and I had never heard her voice so frantic. Subconsciously, I knew focusing on Faith's issues would also distract me from all of the insanity going on in my world.

"He doesn't want me alone today, and I can't blame him. Besides that, it's time for me to learn more about Thomas Hall since I'm going to be living here."

Noah, who was already out of bed, showered and dressed for the day, leaned over and kissed my shoulder, which was left bare from my spaghetti-strap nightgown. When he did, the skin under his lips tingled, and I smiled.

"Okay, ladies. You win," Noah said with a small smile. "We'll be there soon, Faith."

"Thanks," Faith said, not waiting for a response but ending the call. Noah turned to me.

"Are you sure you're up for this?"

"Yes. I'm a little restless this morning. It will be good to get out of the house."

In reality, I was exhausted and didn't want to leave our bed. I was safe within the walls of our home, but I wasn't going to allow that morning's paranoia to affect his career.

I crawled out of bed and spent a few minutes getting ready for the day. Jeans, a tank top, and one of Noah's hundred sweatshirts, along with tennis shoes, seemed perfect for the weather. After a cup of tea and some avocado toast with bacon, Noah, and I headed out the door.

The bright sun and cloudless sky had me longing for a pair of sunglasses, something I no longer owned. When I returned to the house, I needed to start a list of items to replace. Between getting married and being hospitalized, I had yet to begin replacing the things that I had begun to accumulate over the years since leaving California. The visit to Zoe's shop had been a great start, but there were other things I would want to reacquire. Thinking about using the American Express card tickled my brain.

We walked hand-in-hand until we met Faith halfway down the path to the main winery building. After the morning greetings, we turned and headed into the fields. Noah explained to me as we walked that the first month after bud break, when the vines first bloomed, was the most critical time of the season in terms of growth. Climate factors during this *Grand Period of Growth* could make or break a harvest.

Every vine was wrecked. Broken, bent, or battered beyond saving. There wasn't much to begin with because of the April frost, but what was left had been beaten by the chunks of ice that had fallen.

I pulled my phone from my back pocket and googled hail damage in Virginia with the previous day's date. The photos were mind-boggling and included one taken by Cassandra and posted on Thomas Hall's website. The well-taken photograph showed a broken grapevine with at least two inches of ice chunks surrounding it.

I knew nothing about grapes and winemaking, but even I knew this was catastrophic. I listened as Noah and Faith spoke. Before long, we were joined by Cassandra and Alex.

Two hours later, we were still in the fields, but I was over it. I was bored, and it was depressing to see all the beautiful vines and fruit destroyed. I walked over to Noah, took his hand, and squeezed it.

"I'm going to go for a proper walk and let you do your job. Maybe I'll go see Gran."

"Paige, are you sure you're okay? I mean, after yesterday."

I smiled, stood on my toes, and gave him a quick kiss. "I'll be fine. I just feel like I'm in the way here. Today is not the day for me to tag along with you."

He gave me a hug and kissed my forehead before he responded. "I'll call you when I'm done for the day. Okay?"

I nodded and then turned and walked back to the path. I was nearly out of earshot when Alex said, "That marriage of convenience turned very real, very, very fast."

"Convenience? Excuse me?" Noah wasted no time responding, his voice sharp. "The timing may have been convenient, but this marriage is one hundred percent real. For both of us. Don't ever fucking forget it."

"Okay, dude. Sorry. I didn't know."

As I meandered down the path, I thought about what had been said. Marrying Noah had not only been a means to try to quell Vlad's perceived entitlement to me, but it was also very real. It seemed not all of Noah's family understood this fact. I hadn't told Noah I loved him since the shooting—not in so many words. Maybe I needed to start saying it and in front of the family as well.

I watched from a distance as Noah's grandmother made her way to the greenhouse with a few repairmen, so I followed her there. When I reached the door, she was supervising the replacement of multiple panes of glass that the hail had either cracked or shattered.

"Paige, dear, how lovely to see you out and about. Be careful of the glass on the ground. Noah would have my head on a stake if anything else happened to you."

After finding a pair of purple gardening gloves, I cautiously moved around the greenhouse and picked glass out of Vivian's plants. She definitely had a green thumb. I knew a fair bit about plants, having worked at a garden center in Nashville. I was surprised to find so many that were toxic and none were weeds. They mirrored many that were in the new flower beds by the gazebo that Vivian had decided to make a permanent part of Thomas Hall. Had she intentionally created a poison garden?

Within an hour, the greenhouse was repaired and the only broken glass left was on the ground. I had my hand on the handle of the broom when she stopped me.

"You shouldn't be doing that. I know the doctor has you convalescing for a few more weeks. Besides, I can get a member of the staff to do that."

While I was perfectly capable of sweeping and would have argued the point with Noah, I would not argue with Gran. She was the head of the Baker family, and I would never disrespect her wishes. Obeying Alexei Orlov felt like submission because it was but following Vivian Baker's wishes was a matter of respect for a woman who had earned it.

Arm in arm, we slowly made our way back to the house. We settled in the sunroom and Vivian ordered soup, sandwiches, and salads to be sent in.

"I know it's a little early for lunch, but we are training some new staff today, so it might take a while."

"Did something happen with your staff?"

"No, but three are retiring later in the year. This will get the new staff settled in before the older ones retire."

"Makes sense."

We both looked out the windows and saw Noah and the others still examining the vines.

"It's not looking good out there, is it?" she asked.

"Faith said there may not be anything to bottle this year. She thinks the vineyard's crop will be a total loss."

"It's not the first time it's happened."

"Really?"

"It was ages ago. About a decade before Edward met Cassandra."

"Faith's dad?"

"Yes, my son. May God rest his soul. A hurricane tore through the area about two weeks before the harvest. We had so few grapes we couldn't even sell them. We gave them away to anyone who was willing to drive out and pick them. Nothing was fenced in back then. We put an ad in the paper, and in two days, the little that was here was gone."

"How did the winery survive?"

"We had to cut back. I imagine they will this year, too. They will have to lay off some of the staff until next spring."

"I think I will just volunteer not to work until they need me, and even then I can volunteer my services. That would save a salary for someone who needs it. As long as I have a roof over my head and food to eat, I'll be fine."

I hated the thought of not having a paycheck, but it was the right thing to do.

"I think we can manage that," Vivian said with a smile and then paused as though to consider something before speaking again. "Paige, if you could do anything you wanted, what would you do?"

"I've been thinking about that a lot lately. I've thought about college, but my mind keeps going back to an idea I had in New Orleans. A tearoom and tarot shop. I don't know how well that would go over here, though."

"I think if you did private events as well as public openings a few days a week, it would go over well."

"Really?"

Vivian smiled. "Yes, really." I was amazed that she was interested in my aspirations. No one since Genevieve ever thought my dreams were possible. "So, talk to me about this tearoom idea."

We spent the next forty minutes discussing possible locations, what I thought it should look like, and how it would operate.

When I was in New Orleans, tearooms were open daily with up to four seatings. Catering to tourists kept them constantly busy. Gran and I agreed I would need a different approach. Two seatings daily, Thursday through Sunday, starting at four on weekdays and one on weekends. Other times could be reserved for private events.

Ten minutes into our discussion, Vivian left the room and returned with a notebook and pen for me to take notes. When she did, I realized this was no longer a hypothetical situation. She intended to help me get this business up and running.

Chapter Twenty-One

W E WERE JUST WRAPPING up the first of what would be many discussions about The Tea & Tarot Tearoom when our lunch arrived.

Two women came in with trays for us. When they did, I did a double take. One was Miss Judy. I knew her mostly from the wedding as she attended to the bridesmaids that day, but her face had been a presence at Thomas Hall since before I moved to Willow Creek.

It was the person accompanying her that shocked me. The other was a small, thin woman, who, at first glance, looked like my mother. Blinking hard and refocusing my eyes, I realized that the woman was too young to be her. She was so young, in fact, that I should have called her a girl. The shape of her face, blue eyes, and blonde hair were features I knew well. They mirrored my own.

"Irena? Or Elana? Is that really you?"

The question came with a shallow breath and a disorienting lightheadedness. I never thought I would see either of my twin half-sisters again. The last time I'd laid eyes on them, they were so young that I would never be able to tell them apart now.

"Petya? Oh my god! It's Irena." Her voice sounded like that of a bad actress, and she stretched every word. She sat the tray down and ran into my arms. Though wanting to embrace her, something unsettling crept into my brain, and I hesitated, stepping back at her tears. "You even recognized which sister I was after all these years!"

I hadn't. I couldn't tell them apart when they were five. There was no way of knowing who was who after so long.

"No one calls me Petya anymore. It's Paige Foster now. Why are you here?"

"I ran away from Ferma. I couldn't take it anymore."

"And how did you end up in Virginia?"

"I hitchhiked east and met a nice couple who offered to bring me to Virginia. I stayed in Richmond for a while. Then I made my way here and landed this job."

I turned to Vivian. "Did you know? Did you know you hired my half-sister?"

"I didn't hire her. The kitchen manager hires his own staff."

I turned back to Irena. "Did you know Vlad's dead? Alexei is close by, too."

I expected Irena to be shocked by this information, but she wasn't. She struggled but squeezed tears from her eyes. At first, I wanted to believe her reaction was real, but soon realized it was too orchestrated, too phony.

"If Father finds us, he will kill us," Irena said.

Vivian spoke up. "We won't allow that to happen, dear. I'm going to step out of the room and make some calls. Have a seat and eat something with your sister. I imagine y'all have a lot of catching up to do."

Once Vivian was out of the room, we sat and ate. The cucumber sandwiches at Thomas Hall were the best I had ever eaten. I flipped the notebook open and made a note to myself to get the recipe from the cook. Then I focused my attention on my sister.

The last time I laid eyes on her, she was five. Now, she was eighteen and looked so much like our mother. We both did.

"How's Mom?" I asked.

"Mother's dead," she said, and I took a deep breath to let that sink in. "Father caught that evil sin plague that struck a couple of years ago when he went out to sell produce. He survived, but Mom got it from him, and she didn't. Father said it only killed the wicked."

A small wave of sadness overtook me. My mother was no longer alive and hadn't been for a few years. A sin plague? It took me a moment to figure out what she was talking about.

"It wasn't a sin plague. It was probably COVID-19. Millions of people died from it. Even infants, and they aren't wicked. They're babies."

"Well, that's what Father says."

When she said that, I realized that she wasn't a survivor who ran away. She was a zealot, a true believer. Just like Mom.

Her words stuck in my head. *That's what Father says.* It was a phrase, one of many, that was often repeated at Ferma. I had gone to great lengths to strike every phrase from the cult out of my vocabulary immediately upon leaving. Hearing it again made me nauseous, and I felt weak.

I had questions of my own, so I maintained my seemingly calm outward composure and began.

"What did Mom and Alexei tell you about me when I left?"

People rarely left the Orlov cult, so I had no clue how they would spin it.

"Dad told us you were an evil sinner, so a demon came and snatched you away to be his concubine."

"And you believed that?"

"We were five. Of course we did. It made Elana and I stay on our best behavior so we wouldn't get snatched up, too."

"What about Elana, your sister? What happened to her."

"Petya, she's *our* sister."

"It's Paige. And yeah, I guess. How is she?"

"Little Miss Baby Maker?" Jealousy laced her voice with the whiny tone of a brat. "She's too pregnant to travel. She will be having her third baby soon. She keeps poppin' babies out. She already has two boys. She is so lucky."

Having children was truly a blessing under the right circumstances—but three children at eighteen? That was wrong. But knowing she was too pregnant to travel? That didn't add up with escaping the cult that was Ferma.

"Who's the father?"

"Yuri. After you left, Yuri married Polina. She died seven years later, trying to give birth to their fourth child. By that time, my sister and I were thirteen. Father matched us. She went to Yuri. I went to Vlad."

My stomach roiled, knowing what these grown men were doing to children.

"I am so sorry."

"Why are you sorry? I just want babies like my sister. I hope that . . ." She paused, as if she were stopping herself from saying the wrong thing. "I hope that, someday, I get to have babies of my own."

She wasn't at Thomas Hall to earn a paycheck and survive—she hadn't escaped. The questions remained: Why exactly was she there? She had seemed shocked to hear Alexei was in town and surprised to see me, but was she? Or had she been planted there by the family to watch me?

As I searched in awkward silence for where to take the conversation, Gran returned.

"Young lady, it's Irena, isn't it?" She nodded before Gran continued. "If you wish to stay at Thomas Hall, rooms are available in the dorms. We normally only allow the farmhands to stay there, but they are mostly empty this time of year."

She hesitated, trying to form a thought.

"Thank you, but I'm staying at the women's homeless shelter that Catholic Charities has in town. I'm sure I'll be safe there."

Gran gave me a perplexed look. I shook my head. So, she didn't question Irena or push the issue.

"Irena, why don't you go back to work? We'll talk again soon," I said.

She smiled and hugged me before leaving. Once again, I didn't return the hug. Those who lived at Ferma were encouraged to avoid physical contact except when having sex.

As she turned to walk back to the kitchen, Noah came into the room, stopping dead in his tracks when he saw her.

"She's related to you?" he asked after she left the room.

"Yes, my half-sister. Something weird is going on. Let's sit, and I'll explain everything."

Noah and I were preparing for bed as I thought about the strange day. I was holding a bottle of lotion in my hand but had not used it. He took it from me and poured a small amount of lotion on my leg before he began to rub it in. The loving act took me away from my thoughts, and I smiled at him. Noah loved touching my body, and I loved when he touched it. Whenever he had the chance, he would take it. That night, he rubbed lotion on my legs and arms, and his strong hands moving along my skin made me want things from him that I never thought I would.

He said nothing until he finished the second leg and moved onto my arm, all the while keeping his eyes glued to my skin.

"Seeing your half-sister rattled you, didn't it?"

"Yeah."

"I mean, what are the odds she'd end up at Thomas Hall?" he asked.

"I don't think this is happenstance. She's still spouting the rhetoric we were taught growing up. That doesn't mesh with running away. It also makes me wonder if Vlad, Alexei, and Irena all came to Willow Creek at the same time."

"Should we dismiss her? One call to Gran, and she's gone."

"No, what is it that Sun Tzu wrote? 'Keep your friends close and your enemies closer.' I'm not sure which Irena is, but if she's here most days, I can keep an eye on her."

"We all can." He moved on to the second arm, slowly and gently rubbing lotion into my skin.

"You like doing that, don't you?" I asked, placing my free hand on top of his. He froze. "Don't stop. I like it, too."

"If you take your nightgown off, I'll do your back."

"And what about my front?" I asked with a smirk.

"I'll leave that for you to decide." He set the lotion on the nightstand, and within moments, his mouth was on my neck, and I was being laid back onto the mattress.

We spent another of what seemed like a stream of endless evenings together in bed. His lips were warm and wet on my lips, neck, and chest. His hands were soft but strong, and each movement was done with caring intention. He didn't push for anything more, as I was still recovering from the gunshot wounds. I was no fool, though. I knew he was working to help me find my comfort zone before agreeing to give myself to him.

Chapter Twenty-Two

NEITHER NOAH NOR I were shocked when Chief Hayes called us to the station to make statements concerning Vlad's death. It poured rain as we rode in the back of the limo, heading into town. Noah's nervousness manifested itself in the bounce of his leg.

"He's going to find out the truth," Noah said.

"No, he won't. You were asleep at home the whole time. Deny anything else. If you don't, I could end up in jail."

"You want to know the one thing that is really fucked up about all of this?"

"There's only one thing?" I asked, and he gave me a half-hearted smile.

"I didn't do it." It was the first time I had heard him say it, and I let out a deep breath. "Did you think I did it?"

"No, not really. But you never know what someone is capable of doing."

At first, he looked angry but then his face settled into an expression of understanding.

"With the life you've lived, babe, I can't imagine you feeling any other way."

Only moments later, the limo stopped in front of the police station. One bodyguard opened the car door while the other led us into the station. Noah held a golf umbrella over us, and as we walked, I scanned my surroundings. When I did, I saw Alexei standing half a block away, staring me down with his sinister, plastic smile glued to his face. I gripped Noah's arm harder and kept walking as I spoke.

"I just saw Alexei Orlov," I whispered to him under my breath.

"He won't touch you here. Not at a police station."

Once we were through the door and in the lobby, the police chief came out to greet us. He wasted no time with pleasantries. He was all business.

"Paige, I'd like to speak to you first. Noah, you can wait here."

"We can't go back together?" he asked.

"Not right now."

Noah kissed my temple and released the arm he had wrapped around me. Once he did, he rolled his shoulder.

Once we were back in the chief's office, he closed the door. He had a mini fridge behind his desk.

He opened it, grabbed a bottle of water, and offered me one as well. I nodded at the offer, and he handed me one. Only after taking a large gulp did he start asking questions.

"Why did you lie?"

How had he known?

"What do you mean, sir?"

I didn't try to act dumb but wanted to remain polite.

He said nothing but turned his laptop to face me and pushed play. What I saw was black-and-white grainy video footage of a gas station pump. A Mustang pulled up to it, a man exited the car, and began pumping gas. A man I knew well. He rolled his bad shoulder as the gas pumped. It was my husband. But I would never admit it. Not in a million years.

"What am I looking at?" I asked.

"Video footage from a Wawa the night of Vlad Orlov's murder. The timestamp puts this person close to the scene at the right time. And the detective in charge of the case thinks the man in the video is Noah Foster."

"That's not my husband. Can't be. He was asleep next to me."

"So, you don't think it's him? It looks like his car."

"No disrespect, but Ford manufactured a lot of Mustangs. Did you get a plate number?"

"The camera is at the wrong angle."

"Why do you think I'm lying to you, then?"

"I know Noah goes out on late-night rides when he's stressed. I've seen him out and about before. I know Vlad shooting you at your wedding would have been enough for any man to want to kill the guy who tried to kill his bride. And lastly, I know that day in front of the diner, he threatened to put Vlad's dead body in a dumpster if he ever came near you again. Which he did when he shot you."

As Chief Hayes spoke, I suddenly knew, without a doubt, that Noah did not kill Vlad.

"Chief, I know my husband is innocent."

"To be honest, Paige, I don't care who killed the bastard. In my opinion, every misogynist cult member should be lined up and shot."

"That would have been every man over the age of six where I grew up." When I gazed into his eyes, I saw an undeniable sadness. I had a good idea of the answer to the question I was about to ask. "Why do you feel so strongly about this?"

His head dropped, and he closed his eyes as he exhaled hard. After a moment, he raised his head and opened his eyes.

"I had a cousin. Her name was Cherry. She was born with red hair and was three months older than me. She and her parents lived next door to us. Our moms were sisters."

"We were thick as thieves as kids. Always riding our bikes around the neighborhood, building Legos, playing board games on rainy days. You invited one of us somewhere, you'd better assume we'd both be there."

I watched the smile on his face from these happy memories slowly disappear as he continued his story.

"When she was sixteen, she got mixed up with a guy that was in a cult. Four months later, she got pregnant. My aunt begged her to stay at the house with her and my uncle, but she ran off with the guy to live at the compound with him. She died giving birth three months after she left."

Brian closed his eyes and shook his head. After a moment, he continued his story.

"They threw her body in a ditch outside the compound. Her dead baby was still attached to her. The coroner thinks she'd been in the ditch for at least four days before she was found. However, the police said they didn't have enough evidence to prove the cult played any part in her death."

I reached across the desk and rested my hand on his, which probably wasn't appropriate, but I didn't care. The man was in pain, and I understood why. During my time at Ferma, I saw this story play out more than once, minus throwing them in a ditch. There, the dead mother and child would get buried in the bone field with the rest. It wasn't a cemetery. There were no grave markers. It was a field where random holes would be dug, bodies dumped, and the holes covered.

"I am so sorry."

"Thank you. You know, it's been over forty years, and the pain is as fresh as it was when it happened. It's one of the many reasons I became a cop."

"You should probably know something, then."

"What's that?"

"Alexei Orlov is in Willow Creek. I saw him when we were walking into the police station. He was about half a block from here. He was probably the guy who bailed Vlad out. He's Vlad's father."

"And head of Ferma and the Orlov cult." I nodded, and he flipped the laptop facing back to him and typed away. "It says here that an Alexander Jones posted Vlad's bond with an Alaska driver's license."

"He may have had a fake ID. It wouldn't shock me if he killed Vlad."

"He'd kill his son?"

"Vlad was supposed to be the golden child. Next in line to control things. But he was dumb as a tree stump, over forty, and had no children. Vlad's one job was to marry me so Alexei could get access to my trust fund. He failed at that, too, and nearly killed me in the process. Alexei has no patience for that kind of idiocy."

"You believe he did it?"

"He could have, but I know my husband didn't."

"Why are you so certain Noah didn't? And if you say, 'because he was sleeping next to me' again, I'll have you arrested for perjury."

"Because Noah has a serious shoulder injury. He can't lift his arm completely over his head. How would he be able to lift a two-hundred-and-fifty-pound man put him inside a dumpster?"

Chief Hayes leaned back in his chair and relaxed. This was the information he'd been looking for the whole time. He didn't want to charge Noah with murder, and the evidence was stacking up against him. He wanted something to clear Noah's name.

"How long has Noah had this issue?" he asked with a smile.

He knew the answer but just wanted confirmation. But I could do better, could lead him to proof.

"He's had issues and surgeries on his shoulder since long before we met. Ben Sutton has been working with him since before we were married to help him strengthen his shoulder muscles."

"And Ben would attest to this?"

"I don't see why not."

Chief Hayes pulled up a file on his computer and printed it out. After, he stood. "Come on. We're almost done."

I followed him back to the lobby, where we found Noah pacing. When he saw us, he walked across the lobby, meeting us halfway.

"I'm assuming it's my turn now."

"Not exactly." The chief handed him the paper and a pen. "I need you to fill this out so Ben can release your medical records. If the records say what your wife just told me, we can clear you of any suspicion in the murder of Vlad Orlov."

Noah wasted no time filling out the form and handing it back to him.

It wasn't until we were back in the limo that I told him the details of my meeting with the police chief.

"You mean to tell me that he had me on camera, and you still said I was asleep next to you?"

"Yes, and while I was talking my way out of it, I realized you couldn't lift Vlad over your head to put him in a dumpster."

Noah smiled and shook his head. "Smart and beautiful. I'm a lucky man."

Chapter Twenty-Three

"PAIGE, DEAR, WHAT ARE you doing right now?" Noah's grandmother asked after I hit the speaker button on my phone and said hello.

I rubbed the sleep from my eyes and glanced at the clock on the fireplace mantle. It was a little after one in the afternoon. I didn't want to admit she had woken me from a two-hour nap.

Healing from a gunshot wound took a lot of energy, and while the external injuries were repairing fast, the internal damage was taking longer.

"Nothing special. Getting ready to make myself a sandwich."

"Why don't you come eat lunch at my house? I have something I would like to show you."

As she spoke, Paco jumped into my lap, demanding scratches under the chin.

I was still tired, but I found it hard to say no to the family matriarch.

"Give me about fifteen minutes, and I'll be there."

"Bring your tarot cards and your tearoom notebook, too."

It hadn't taken me long to learn not to question Gran's requests or orders. There was always a method to what often seemed random or madness. It was easier just to follow her directions and see where it took you.

When I arrived, Hope was sitting with Gran in the library, looking over maps and blueprints. Jazz filled the rooms through the speakers hidden in the walls, and it reminded me of the music in New Orleans.

Hope met me halfway across the floor and embraced me in a long hug. Something was different about her. I scanned her from head to toe, and it took a second to realize what I was seeing and feeling.

Hope was pregnant.

She and Grayson had only been married a little over a month.

My thoughts must have shown in my expression. Hope quietly shook her head. No one knew yet. At least no one but Grayson. The two kept no secrets from each other.

I gave a slow nod, confirming I understood her silent request.

"What are you and Gran looking at?"

"Properties in town I own. I'm hoping one will be suitable for your tearoom. Gran says there will be tarot readings, too. I didn't know you did that."

"Yeah, I thought you knew. I do readings for Faith a lot."

"Really? I never pictured her as the type who would enjoy that."

Hope and Faith had an unusual relationship. As sisters, they loved each other. However, Hope constantly made assumptions about her shy sister that simply weren't true. Until recently, Faith had held her tongue to keep the peace, but after returning home from college, she found her voice and called Hope out on her foolishness.

"She actually finds it fascinating." As I continued, Hope rolled her eyes. "Would you like me to read yours?"

"Maybe later. Let's take a look at some locations for your tearoom," Hope said dismissively.

I wasn't sure if she was hesitant to look at her future or thought it all was silly. She was a complex woman to read.

However, Gran had other ideas.

"Lunch first. Then, we'll discuss the tearoom. Or are either of you in a hurry?"

I shook my head, and Hope opened her phone.

"Believe it or not, I have nothing this afternoon. Maybe I'll text Gray to come here after work."

"Y'all could have dinner with me and Noah. I could invite Faith and Ben, too. If you and your sister are speaking this week."

"As far as I know, we are. You'll have to check with her. Ever since she and Ben got together, she's changed. I just don't understand her anymore. She acts so headstrong."

"I'll text her."

I knew why Faith was behaving the way she did. Ben had given her the confidence to stand up for herself, and Hope could be bossy and overbearing where her sister was concerned.

"Let me check with Gray as well. It sounds like a fun night." As her fingers flew across her phone, Gran called the kitchen to have lunch set up in the sunroom as we made our way in that direction.

A few minutes later, Irena brought in a tray of salads and bread, followed by two other employees who brought iced tea and fruit. After the trays were laid, Vivian informed the staff I was throwing a dinner party that night and would need to talk to the chef about the menu.

When the three left the room, Irena stayed behind. I was sure she lingered with big doe eyes, hoping to be asked to join us. However, she needed to understand that the other day was the exception, not the rule. So, with the exclusion of a slight nod, I didn't acknowledge her presence, and after a few seconds, she gave up and headed back to the kitchen.

The three of us sat, enjoying the Cobb salads and freshly baked rolls alone with iced tea. We didn't linger at lunch but ate before returning to the library and attacking the task at hand. However, I didn't realize how it would all play out.

There were four locations on the map sprawled across the table, and the three of us stood over the map and its markings. Two were on Main Street: the old drug store and a bank that closed before I moved to town. The third building was across the street from the bowling alley and was a failed sandwich shop. The last location was on Seventh Street, two blocks from the Victorian home Faith was renovating. It was a home that had been re-zoned for commercial use.

Both women had opinions on locations but so did I. Three years before, the drugstore on Main Street relocated into the building where the kids' clothing store once stood. The owner retired and closed the store when no one wanted to buy it. The old drugstore was across the street from Zoe's shop, next to the jewelry store and not far from the florist. It made for a nice "girly" block of shops.

I also liked the idea of being on Main Street. Visibility would be good for a new place in Willow Creek, and I had concerns that no one would notice it if it weren't on Main Street.

"The old drugstore it is, then," Hope said as she pulled out her phone and made a call.

I turned to Gran.

"This all sounds great in theory, but how would I go about renting it?" I watched as Hope whispered into the phone. "What is she up to, anyway?"

"Arranging your wedding gift. She owns that building. It's about to be yours."

"What? That's crazy!"

Hope was off the phone and turned back in our direction.

"Done. In about four weeks, you will own the building that used to be the drugstore. You'll have to let me know if I should put the deed in just your name or yours and Noah's."

I dropped into a nearby chair as I gasped for air.

"Hope," I said, inhaling between words. "You buy people household appliances as wedding gifts, not buildings."

"Do you need appliances?"

"No."

I couldn't believe she asked me that.

"Do you want appliances?"

"No."

Hope knew that wasn't the point of my statement.

"Correct. What you need is a building. Now you have one."

I leaned over and dropped my head between my knees, focusing on my breathing until it regulated itself. When I sat up, Gran and Hope were smiling at me. Apparently, Hope texted Noah and informed him I was on the verge of a panic attack. He arrived just as I was beginning to regain my composure.

Within a fraction of a second, he was on his knees in front of me. An easy smile and bright eyes stared back at me.

"Are you okay?"

I nodded and whispered, "Did Hope tell you about the wedding gift?"

"Yes, and I think it's a brilliant idea. I called my lawyer on the walk over." He turned to Hope. "Put it in her name only. It will be her business, not mine."

"No," I said. "Everything that is mine is yours."

He had said this to me so many times since we married. It was good to toss the statement back to him.

"We'll talk about that later. You need a postnup for your trust, too. We should have handled that before the wedding."

"But—"

"I promised to protect you. And I will. In every way possible. Including financially. There are accounts we'll share, but businesses need defined boundaries. Just like my Thomas Hall Winery shares will remain mine, your tearoom will be all yours."

"Noah?"

The whisper of his name had quickly become my fallback statement when I was completely overwhelmed and desperately in need of his assistance.

He wrapped his arms around me, pulling me from my seat so I could lean against his chest.

"Gran and your cousin are crazy," I whispered. "Isn't this getting a little ridiculous? It's all too much. Why is your family so extra?"

His arms wrapped tighter around me, and I felt the vibration in his chest when he chuckled. All seemed right in the world when he held me.

I was about to suggest he take the remainder of the day off when his cell phone rang. He pulled it from his pocket and answered. When he hung up, he lightly brushed his lips across mine.

"Sorry, babe. I've got to go back to work for a while. Why don't you spend the rest of the afternoon here, and I'll come back for you when the day is done."

"Before you go, I, um, kinda, invited Hope, Grayson, Faith and Ben to dinner tonight. I hope that's okay. I guess I should have asked you first."

"Okay? Of course it's okay." He leaned down and kissed me. "I love that you want to spend time with my family. I guess it would be better to meet you at the house after work instead."

I nodded, and he placed one more kiss on my forehead.

"I'll walk you out," Hope said, not giving anyone else a chance.

Once she was out of the room, I turned to Gran.

"Hope doesn't just give away real estate. How much of your hand and pocketbook are in this?"

Gran grinned. "I reserve the right not to answer that question. But I have one for you."

"What's that?" I asked.

"How pregnant do you think Hope is, and does she know?"

I wondered how she knew and grinned. "She knows. She's not ready to tell the world yet, though. My guess is somewhere between eleven and thirteen weeks."

"I was thinking the same."

"Do you want children?"

"Yes. I would like one or two. Noah seems to like the idea as well. I don't think we'll wait too long to start. I'm nearly thirty. I just have to get cleared at my post-op visit first."

"Cleared for what?" Hope asked as she entered the room.

"Baby making," Gran said matter-of-factly.

"Oh. What's next?" Hope asked, obviously hoping to change the subject.

"Come with me, ladies," Gran said.

Hope and I followed her, and she led us to the dining room. All of her furniture had been removed, and antiques filled the room. There were no beds or large dressers but tons of tables, chairs, desks, paintings, planters, mirrors and cabinets.

"Paige, this is all furniture from my attic. You are welcome to anything you like for the tearoom or your house."

I looked around the huge room, overwhelmed by my options. How was I ever going to decide?

"But what about your other grandchildren? Shouldn't they have a look before me?"

"They already have. How do you think Faith's house will get decorated? She's already pulled what she wants, and we've put it in storage near the Victorian she's renovating."

I walked through the furniture three times before I could begin to even think about making any decisions. It was overwhelming. Gran noticed my stress level rising, handed me a stack of Post-It notes, and I used them for furniture labeling. I marked two pieces I wanted to be delivered to the house. The rest would almost completely furnish the tearoom.

"You've made lovely choices," Gran said.

"It's probably more than will fit in the space, but it's all so beautiful."

"I'll have it stored in town until you are ready for it."

"Thank you."

"Next time, we'll look at china tea services. You will need a lot, and we found so many in the attic. This is becoming a brilliant way to purge the extra stuff here at the house."

Chapter Twenty-Four

THE FOLLOWING FRIDAY NIGHT, Noah's friends and their dates started arriving around six. When our guests first arrived, Paco greeted them in the den, demanding affection. When the numbers grew, though, he made his way upstairs, away from the noise. I didn't blame him. I was nervous and beginning to think the party wasn't a great idea, but I relaxed when I saw Faith and Ben arrive, along with a few other familiar faces.

Larry, whom I had seen at Hope's reception but had never been introduced to, greeted me with a big hug as though we had known each other for ages. I was uncomfortable being hugged by a complete stranger, but I rapidly discovered that most of Noah's friends were huggers. Larry didn't bring a date, but most of Noah's other friends had.

The guys all seemed thrilled that Noah had gotten married. However, the women brought preconceived opinions of me. On the surface, they were syrupy sweet, but I heard whispers of words like "gold digger" and even questions if I was baby-trapping him early in the evening.

I ignored the whispers and stayed close to Noah as we worked the room together. He would introduce me to a couple, tell me how he knew them, and then bring up a topic I could contribute to. The majority of the guys were fraternity buddies from his days in college. Noah had pledged his Uncle Edward's frat, Kappa Sigma, and had even gotten a tattoo on the back of his left shoulder that was similar to his uncle's.

As Chris, a frat buddy who played basketball with Noah in college, told me a funny story about traveling to a post-season game, I glanced over and saw a tall, lanky man staring at Faith. He looked forlorn when Ben wrapped his arm around her.

As the night progressed, we spent time with all of Noah's friends. It didn't take long for most of them to understand my marriage to Noah wasn't about his money but about wanting to build a life together.

It was nearly seven when the last of Noah's friends arrived. His name was Morty, and he had a surprisingly familiar guest. I walked over to greet them, and Noah, who had been on the other side of the room, joined me. He wrapped an arm protectively around my waist when I reached them.

"Hi, Irena," I said, tension filling my body.

"Oh, so you know my date?" Morty asked.

"We share a mother," I said before turning to her. I was nervous enough, trying to make a good impression on Noah's friends without my past invading my present. "What are you doing here?"

"Morty asked me out. When he said we were coming to a party here, I didn't think you'd mind."

I raised an eyebrow before glancing at Noah, who was studying my expression when Morty spoke up.

"Why do I get the feeling I just stirred some family drama? Should we leave?"

"No, Morty. Any friend of Noah's is a friend of mine. As for my half-sister, we were recently reunited after being kept apart for a dozen years. Things are a little awkward between us right now, but I'm sure we'll adjust."

"Drinks are on the patio," Noah said to them. "Go help yourself."

Irena smiled as she walked away, arm-in-arm with Morty. It was a plastic smile that left me uneasy. It reminded me of her father's mischievous smirk.

"Are you sure you want her here?" Noah whispered as he held me in his arms, and his lips grazed my ear.

"I'm not going to cause a scene in front of your friends." Before I could say more, he leaned in and kissed me until I was unsteady on my feet.

"Okay, you two. That's enough of that," Hope said as she made her way to us. She had a bottle of root beer in her hand instead of her usual whiskey and was holding Grayson's hand with the other.

Grayson was one of the brewery's brewmasters. He was protective of Hope, and I could only imagine how her pregnancy was going to amplify that.

The guys shook hands as Hope and I hugged. They had come around the same time Faith and Ben had arrived. We were greeting other guests at the time and hadn't had a chance to say hello.

Noah had insisted I invite some of my friends. However, most were related to him. I had invited all of his cousins, his sister, and a couple of Hope's bridesmaids to join us.

"I just saw your sister," Hope commented. "She keeps popping up everywhere. I saw her in Zoe's shop, getting her hair trimmed. Her hair is crazy long."

"Yeah, Zoe told me she met her at Gran's and offered to trim up the split ends."

Hope chuckled. "Aunt Zoe can't stand to see someone walking around with bad ends. It drives her nuts."

"She didn't know Irena was my sister until they were talking while she was sitting in Aunt Zoe's chair."

"Wow!" Noah said. "Aunt Zoe is usually pretty observant. I wonder how she missed that?" He ran his fingers through my hair as he spoke.

"Was your hair ever that long?"

"Mine was longer when I lived at Ferma. One of the first things I did when I escaped was cut fourteen inches off. The hairdresser that did it donated the hair to an organization that makes wigs for kids with cancer."

"I'm surprised she didn't do the same."

Grayson and Noah, who were now both listening to us, looked concerned.

"You don't think she ran away, do you?" Grayson asked.

"I wanted to believe she had escaped. The more I interact with her, though, the more I think she's been told to follow me and watch what I'm doing using any means necessary."

"So, what are you going to do?" Hope asked.

"Watch her right back."

I was going to say more, but the tall, lanky man who had been staring at Faith earlier walked over and shook Noah's hand.

"Thanks for inviting me, Noah," he muttered with a soft voice.

"You're not heading out yet, are you? You haven't even met my wife yet."

Noah turned to me. "Paige, I'd like you to meet Charlie Archer. He's the assistant winemaster at Queen Charlotte Vineyards. Faith and Charlie went to App State together."

"It's nice to meet you," I said as I shook his hand.

"Congratulations," Charlie said to me before turning back to Noah. "Yeah, I'm going to head out. I've had a hell of a week, and—well, you know me—parties aren't really my thing. I appreciate the invite, though."

As he walked away, Hope, who had been standing next to me the whole time, leaned in. and said, "I always thought Faith should have ended up with him. They are the perfect match."

That's when I remembered Faith telling me about Charlie. She referred to him as having the personality of a wet, sandy beach towel. After my brief encounter with him, I understood why she felt that way.

I excused myself and made my way over to Faith and Ben after pouring myself a glass of wine.

"How's my favorite engaged couple?" I asked them.

"Thirsty," Ben said. "I'm going to go get a drink." He turned to Faith after spotting my full glass. "Do you want anything?"

Faith shook her head before he kissed her temple and walked towards the patio.

She turned her attention to me.

"Thanks again for having Ben and me to dinner the other night. We had a lot of fun."

"So did we. Your sister behaved pretty well, too."

"I think Grayson talked to her beforehand. When he does, things seem to go smoother."

"Makes sense. He's definitely a take-charge kind of guy."

I scanned the room before Faith asked, "How do you think the party's going?"

"Okay. I know Noah is enjoying himself. I spent so many years trying not to stand out and be noticed that it's hard to be the center of attention."

"One of the great things about being me is that few people notice me."

"Not true. Charlie Archer was staring at you tonight."

"Ugh. I was hoping he would get over my not wanting to date him. Especially now that I'm engaged."

"Hope is still wishing you'd gone for him."

"He's a nice enough guy, but he's not my type."

"Who's not your type? Not me, I hope?" Ben asked, having returned with a soda in hand.

"You are definitely my type," Faith said as she stood on her toes to kiss him.

While they kissed, I retreated to a quiet spot to process everything before Morty approached, cracking open a beer as he did.

"Are you sure I didn't start something by bringing Irena?"

"No. It's fine. We are just trying to get to know each other. She and her twin sister were only five when I left home."

"Twin?"

He didn't know Irena was one of a matching set.

"Yeah."

"She said y'all grew up on a big farm in California. What was that like?"

I debated on how much to share, but sooner or later, all of Noah's friends would know the truth. That's why I didn't sugarcoat it.

"Well, there was a farm where we grew up, but it was really a cult compound. Did she not tell you her last name?"

"She said it was Olsen and that she's twenty-five," Morty said, looking more and more concerned.

"It's Orlov." I watched as the gears turned in his head until he connected all the dots, and his eyes grew wide. "And, Morty, a word of advice—Irena is barely eighteen and looking to score a baby. So, unless you're ready to be a dad and join a cult so you can see your child, I would tread very carefully."

Morty swallowed hard. The expression on his face told me my warning was a little too late.

The night wound down after eleven until there were only a handful of people left. I was sitting on the floor when Irena stumbled over and plopped herself down next to me. She wrapped an arm around my shoulders.

"You know, sis," she began with a slow, drunken, and slightly slurred voice. "I used to be so jealous of you. I was so in love with Vlad, and he was obsessed with you. 'Petya's lips were fuller.' 'Petya's tits were better.' All day, every day. 'Petya, Petya, Petya.' He barely gave me the time of day."

Every time she called me Petya, I wanted to shrivel up and disappear. I looked across the room and saw Noah talking with Ben. When he saw Irena hanging on me, he gave me a concerned look. He excused himself from his discussion and headed toward Morty.

"He didn't even want to have sex with me. And the whole time we did it, he would complain that I wasn't you."

I didn't know how to answer that, and luckily, I didn't have to.

Morty and Noah came up to us and Morty helped Irena to her feet, holding her steady in her drunken state.

"Come on, cutie. It's time for me to take you home."

"Your home?" Irena asked, smiling.

"Not tonight. You are a little too drunk for that," Morty said, glancing up at me.

He guided her toward the door as Noah helped me to my feet and held me tight. When Irena reached the door, she turned back and said, "Good night, sis. I love you!"

And then they left.

I gave out a sigh of relief, and Noah kissed my forehead before he said, "Some party, huh?"

"Some party indeed."

Chapter Twenty-Five

MONDAY MORNING, NOT LONG after Noah left for work, a limo pulled up to the front door, and two bodyguards emerged. I had a follow-up appointment with the doctor who performed my surgery the day of the shooting.

Noah wanted to attend, but there was a winery board meeting to discuss the upcoming season—or lack thereof—and the best way to proceed. He hated the idea of me leaving Thomas Hall without him and tried to get me to reschedule my appointment. However, I was ready to move forward with my life and wanted to get the appointment handled.

My doctor was impressed with how quickly my injuries healed and praised me for following his orders. The appointment was short, and afterward, when the driver asked me where I wanted to go next, I asked him to take me to the yarn store one town over.

My bodyguards were not thrilled about this but agreed to the shopping trip as long as they stayed close to me. When we arrived,

I left my purse in the car, taking with me only the credit card Noah had given me.

When I was a preteen at Ferma, I learned to knit and crochet. I knitted sweaters during the summer for people on the farm to wear during the winter months. And when it was cold outside, I would crochet market bags for Alexei to sell at the farmer's market on Saturdays. I missed that creative outlet and thought it might help with my restlessness.

An hour later, I left the store, with knitting needles, crochet hooks, a vast variety of yarn and thread, as well as three large baskets to store it all in.

I was sitting on the floor in the den organizing my new purchases when Noah came home for lunch. I was beginning to feel guilty about spending his money on something as frivolous as yarn.

"You went shopping after your appointment?" Noah asked as he leaned over and kissed me.

"Just one store. There's a yarn store one town over, but I may have spent too much. And I used the credit card you gave me."

"How much is too much?" he asked.

I handed him the receipt, and he smiled.

"Babe, this is not too much. It's almost nothing. Most women would be hitting the designer boutiques and charging thousands of dollars."

"So, it's okay?"

He wrapped me in his arms. "Are you happy with what you got?"

"Yes."

"Then, it's fine."

"Are you hungry?" I asked, and he nodded. "Then, let's fix some lunch."

When bedtime finally arrived, I was antsy. I wasn't sure if I was ready for sex, but I wanted to try. Noah deserved it, and if it could be everything most people said it was, so did I.

We went upstairs to the master suite. He hopped into the shower, as he often did before coming to bed. He claimed he needed to wash the winery off of him before climbing under the covers.

I wasted no time stripping down and pulling my hair into a messy bun.

He was barely wet when I opened the shower door open and slipped in with him.

As soon as Noah saw me, his eyes widened. He placed his hands on my shoulders before pulling me close to him.

"Is this okay?" he whispered in my ear.

Leaning against him, I nodded, placing my back to his chest. He wrapped me in his arms, and we stayed that way until I felt comfortable with both of us naked, then turned to face him once more. I placed a kiss on his chest and then another, slightly higher. I continued the pattern until I was on my toes and my mouth was on his.

The rest of the world left my mind, and I only desired one thing: the man in front of me.

My husband.

My friend.

My everything.

I grabbed the shampoo.

"Close your eyes."

He did as he was told, and I massaged the shampoo into his scalp. It was not only relaxing for Noah, but the hot water and steam relaxed me as well.

After I rinsed his hair, I felt a soapy washcloth against my neck. Noah worked it over my body, leaving no spot untouched. Once my skin was rinsed, the water shut off, and I opened my eyes. Noah's face was inches away from mine.

"I'm not done. I was going to wash you."

"Later," he said, his voice was rough and low.

"Okay." It was time for me to say what I had been thinking about all day. "Noah, I'm ready. I want you. All of you. Tonight."

Wordlessly, Noah used a soft, oversized towel to dry me off before wrapping me in it. He quickly dried himself off, picked me up, and carried me to the bed.

Seconds later, I was flat on my back, and Noah hovered over me.

"Are you sure about this?" he asked in a soft, caring tone.

I nodded.

After kissing me deeply, leaving me breathless, his mouth worked its way down my neck onto my breast before giving each nipple attention. My body took over, responding in ways I couldn't have imagined. My back arched, and I mumbled my dissatisfaction when his lips left my breasts.

"Patience, babe," Noah said with a smile as he left a trail of kisses down the center of my abdomen. It wasn't until he worked south beyond my belly button that I understood his plan.

"Noah, uh, I've never had anyone . . . I mean, you don't have to."

He lifted his head, rested his chin on my left thigh and looked into my eyes. He had a smirk on his face and a twinkle in his eyes. "Do you want me to stop?"

A small smile crept onto my warm, flushed face. "No, I don't."

Noah had put a lot of thought into what it would take for me to be present and satisfied, including an ending with me on top and in complete control. It was only when I woke the next morning that I grasped the distinct difference between sex and being made love to by a man who cherished me.

"Paige, babe? Are you hungry?"

I could feel the weight of Noah's body sitting on the edge of the bed, next to me. I opened my eyes to find us nearly nose-to-nose. He leaned in a little closer and greeted me with a sweet kiss.

"What time is it?" I asked when our lips disconnected.

"A little before nine."

I sat up as I spoke. "Shouldn't you be at work?"

"I'll go in after lunch. There's not much to do today, and I wanted to be here this morning, with my wife."

I smiled. I loved when he referred to me as his wife.

"Now, are you ready for breakfast?"

Before I could answer, he was on his feet, and seconds later, there was a bed tray in front of me. On it were pancakes, bacon, fruit, and tea. Everything was stacked high and could easily feed multiple people.

"I am hungry, but this could feed a battle battalion."

"Oh, I'm going to help."

I grabbed a slice of bacon and ate it. "Did you cook?"

"I'd love to lie and say I did." He cut the pancakes as he spoke. "I called up to the main house and this is what they sent."

We sat on the bed and enjoyed our breakfast together. I wasn't sure who enjoyed it more, so I made a mental note that we should do this regularly.

When we were done, Noah moved the tray from the bed before snuggling up to me.

"How are you this morning?"

I turned my head to stare into his beautiful eyes.

"I'm good."

"Yeah?"

"I have to admit, I was nervous last night, but it wasn't bad at all. I kind of enjoyed it."

"Just kind of?"

"Okay, I really enjoyed it." I giggled. "I never thought I would hear myself say that."

"Just wait. It will only get better from here."

Chapter Twenty-Six

"Boring," I said out loud, even though I was in the kitchen alone. I opened a cabinet that stored the tea and was gravely disappointed.

I requested loose tea only, and the kitchen at the main house had complied with my request. However, what they supplied me with, although of the highest quality, was boring. I stared at the tins and pulled out the Darjeeling tea, placing it on the counter. Even though I had not mixed my own tea in ages, I needed something more complex than what was available.

After scouring the spice cabinet and raiding the fruit bowl, I mixed together bits of apple and orange peel, cloves, and a pinch of cinnamon with some of the tea leaves. After making a cup, I added a little more cinnamon. It was perfect. I grabbed my tearoom notebook and wrote it down. I would need a dehydrator to dry the apple and orange peel, but it would make a nice seasonal blend to serve in the tearoom.

I grabbed a basket of crocheting supplies, and along with my tea, I made my way to the patio to enjoy the morning.

It was the perfect day—not too hot yet but not as cold as the day Hope married Grayson. A refreshing breeze allowed the scent of freshly bloomed jasmine to float through the air. Soon, the weather would turn into furnace-level heat with the humidity of a sauna.

After having a second cup of tea while still sitting on the patio and crocheting, my restlessness got the best of me. Over the previous few days, I had noticed a remarkable improvement in my health and energy levels. I decided a walk would be the perfect exercise. It was nearly eleven, and I could surprise Noah at work in time for lunch.

I don't know why, but when I left the house, I didn't follow the path. I walked through the fields of vines, examining the devastation and some areas the field hands had cleaned up in hopes of salvaging the plants for the next year's harvest. From there, I meandered past the greenhouse and through the rows of Vivian's private garden until I came to the security fence that surrounded the estates and winery.

I turned toward the production building, leisurely walking and thinking about the future. The Tea and Tarot was really going to happen. Gran and I had spent the morning before at the main house talking to her finance guy about funding and, at my insistence, paying Vivian back for the startup funding. As I walked, I allowed my fingertips to graze the chain-link fence.

My mind wandered to thoughts of color palettes and menus when a strong hand gripped my fingers and held them between the fence's metal.

"Hello, Petya."

Alexei's deep and heavily Russian-accented voice was unforgettable and had not changed since I was a child.

I pulled my hand away from his, but he squeezed harder, holding me in place. My breathing became quick and shallow.

"Is that any way to greet your papa after such a long time?"

"You are not my father," I said, releasing myself from his grip.

"Now, Petya, why would you say such a thing?"

I pulled my phone out and dialed Brian's number.

"Hello. It's Paige Foster. Better every day. Remember when I told you I thought I knew who killed Vlad? He's standing in front of me. No, there's a fence between us. Perfect. Thank you." I ended the call.

"I won't be here long enough for the police to arrive." Alexei had maybe five minutes. "I knew if I came and circled the fence on a day like today, you would show up eventually. You've seen me at the fence before."

I thought back to my second evening at Thomas Hall, when I caught a glimpse of a man I thought was Vlad.

"You've been here the whole time?"

"Did you really think I would let Vlad travel alone? He's not smart enough to navigate the outside world."

"Oh."

It wasn't until that moment I confirmed my earlier suspicion. Vlad, Alexei, and Irena had traveled together. They had literally come as a group to drag me home.

"Before people start arriving, there are a few things you need to know," he said.

"I know enough about you. You're a money-hungry charlatan who doesn't care for anyone but himself."

"You give me such little credit. I cared enough about your wishes to let you live your life for the last thirteen years."

I knew I should run, but my feet were frozen in place. In addition, I wanted answers.

"What do you mean?"

"After we got word you were in New Orleans, I had a detective follow you to Tennessee and then to Washington, DC. I could have been paying people to watch you here in Willow Creek for the last four years, for all you know."

My stomach churned, and my mind raced. I thought about everyone I met since my move to Willow Creek and if any would have spied on me.

"However, you are about to turn thirty. Now, I will get you back to California and marry you, since Vlad is dead, and take your trust fund. I used all of your mother's money ages ago."

"Then what?" I wondered how far through he had thought his plan through.

"You will make me a baby or two. And then I will kill you just like I killed Vlad. No, not like Vlad. Slower. More painful. Maybe while I fuck you."

I had never seen his grin so sinister.

My body began to shake uncontrollably. I hoped Alexei wouldn't notice. I didn't want him to see the extent of my fear.

"So, it was you."

"But how did you know to drop him in a dumpster so the police would suspect Noah? Wait. He only ever made that threat once. You were at the diner that day?"

"I was in a truck across the street. You were always the smart one. Speaking of, you keep talking to keep me here, but the police won't find me when they arrive."

With that, Alexei turned and walked into the forest, disappearing into the thick brush as golf carts drove up from all directions. Noah was in one of them.

Noah and I sat in his office in the production building. He shared it with Cassandra, but she was mostly retired and only maintained a small desk in a corner. From what I had been told, minus the smaller desk, the office looked pretty much the same as it had been ever since Noah's grandfather, Edward Baker, Sr., ran the winery. A large Oriental rug covered the industrial warehouse floor, and an oversized desk was the focal point of the room. A sofa and side table with a lamp sat in front of a floor-to-ceiling window.

Noah was next to me on the sofa, and I could feel the anger radiating from him.

"Why were you outside?"

His question surprised me.

"Why wouldn't I be?"

"You should have been at home."

"Noah, you keep telling me Thomas Hall is a fortress. Why wouldn't I go for a walk on a day like today? You've spent our entire marriage saying I'm safe as long as I'm at Thomas Hall."

As I told the police officer what had transpired, he listened. Brian wasn't on duty when I called him. He called another officer, the security hut at the gate of Thomas Hall, then Noah before making his way to Thomas Hall anyway. He had a long history with the Baker family, and while I didn't know the details, I was always grateful for his presence.

Noah stared at me, looking angry, so I continued.

"You can't expect me to spend the rest of my life in the house. I'm getting ready to open a tearoom. I'm actually going to have to be there."

"I'm going to have to talk to Gran about that. The tearoom is canceled!"

"Canceled? I don't think so."

"You're only safe if you are here!"

"And you're delusional. I haven't left Thomas Hall today, and I was threatened with kidnapping, forced marriage, rape, and murder. And all of it by a man who doesn't make idle threats."

"But he never got over the fence."

"He'll find a way," I said.

"No, he won't. It's impenetrable."

"And I'm going to say it again: You. Are. Delusional. What makes you think the security here is so perfect?"

"Uncle Edward locked this place down when Aunt Cassandra moved here. He constantly paid for upgrades and improvements until he died."

"And it always had issues. I've heard about them all over the years. I know you loved your uncle. I met him a few of times before he died, and he was a nice guy, but he was far from perfect. If you don't believe me, ask Faith. He was her father, and she saw it all. The greatness of him and his imperfections."

Noah growled at me like an angry dog. I had crossed a line bringing his uncle into the argument.

"Don't ever say that again. He was the greatest man I've ever known."

"I don't doubt that. What I doubt is that he turned Thomas Hall into the perfect bubble of peace and safety you think it is."

"It's close enough to perfect," Noah said, trying to convince me.

"That didn't do Hope much good when she was being stalked."

"That weirdo confronted her at the community center pool."

"But the lunatic was living in the dorms here. Living! At Thomas Hall!"

Noah said nothing. He only stared at me, knowing I was right.

I stood to leave, but only got two steps in when Noah's hand tightened on my wrist.

"Where are you going?"

"Somewhere you're not. I can't deal with you right now."

"Well, I'm not letting you go alone. I need to keep you safe."

I pulled my wrist from his hand and backed away, moving toward the door.

"You are so controlling! So overprotective! It's driving me crazy! I wish, I wish—"

"You wish what?" His voice was deep and raspy. "That we never met? That you never moved to Willow Creek? That we didn't get married?"

My heart sank into my stomach, and tears pooled in my eyes but didn't fall. At that moment, I was certain he was projecting his desires upon me, and my heart ached. I stared at him for a moment before a whisper left my mouth.

"So, that's what you think, huh?"

I didn't wait for his answer before walking from his office and racing down the stairs. When I opened the door to leave the building, I was face-to-face with Faith.

"Paige," she said after only taking a fraction of a second to read my body language. "What's wrong?"

"Your cousin is an asshole. That's what's wrong." I pushed past her and walked down the gravel drive. I hadn't gone far when Zoe and Henry's house appeared on the right and saw Zoe getting out of her car. She was the only member of the family who kept her car parked at her house and not the garage.

She raised her arm and waved. It wasn't until I got closer and she saw my expression of unhappiness that she tilted her head and truly examined me. When I reached her, she hugged me.

"Noah?" Zoe asked.

"Why does he have to be so impossible?"

"Come on in," she said, motioning to the door. "Sounds like you need a break from him."

I followed her into the house. Zoe and Henry's house was a place where people lived. Whereas the main house resembled a museum, their house looked like a home. The throws draped across chairs and the tidy stack of mail on the entry table made me feel better about the state of the house Noah and I were living in. I never left the house messy, but I didn't keep things as precise as Gran's house.

Once I was comfortable in an oversized chair, Zoe handed me a glass of white wine.

"Isn't it a little early in the day for this?"

"It's well after noon, and we live at a winery. Take advantage of it."

I took a few sips of wine. "Is it possible to both hate and love something at once?"

"I'm assuming since you said something that we are not talking about a person."

"No. Noah is exasperating, but I'm not talking about him. It's Thomas Hall."

"I get it. I've lived here for years. The first time as a homeless pregnant teen and then again with Henry, but I didn't make the move permanently until I got pregnant with the twins. Thomas Hall is like living on a different planet. Even now, I keep the apartment above the boutique for myself."

As Zoe spoke, I drank. I didn't know much about Zoe's first child except that he died while serving in the Marines. I didn't know she lived at Thomas Hall when she was pregnant then as well.

"And your case is so crazy. I'm sure you feel like you are living in a gilded cage."

"Isn't that the truth," I said before taking another sip. "It's a wonderful place, but I still feel trapped. And Noah is just so delusional. He gets worse every single day."

"Delusional? How?"

"He thinks nothing bad can happen to me if I just stay in our house and do nothing."

Zoe attempted to snort back a laugh and failed. I raised my glass to my lips and found it empty. She immediately refilled it and topped hers off.

"Yeah. Edward spent a lot of time trying to fortify Thomas Hall to protect Cassandra and the girls. Somewhere along the way, Noah became convinced his uncle was a superhuman who could do no wrong."

"Yeah, I pointed that out in an argument we just had. It may have been an error."

"In the short term, probably. But he needed to hear it. Do you mind if I asked what you argued about?"

I told her the story of my morning and the blow-by-blow of the short but powerful argument Noah and I had in his office. I was finishing off my second glass of wine when there was a knock at the door.

Before Zoe was on her feet, Faith walked into the room with three boxed lunches, and Nora followed her, carrying her own. She had watched me walk into Zoe's house with her and decided to call the main house and arrange for a simple lunch for the three of us.

"Hey, sis," Nora said, giving me a hug before sitting down.

I came home to surprise you for lunch at the main house, but apparently, the party is here.

Faith poured herself and Nora a glass of wine before topping off everyone else's glass and finishing off the bottle. Zoe retrieved another bottle. While she did, I took the box lunch from Faith. A chicken salad sandwich on sourdough bread, baby carrots, melon, and a cookie were waiting in the white box for me. I ate the melon first while drinking my wine before devouring my sandwich.

After half an hour of mindless chatter, Faith turned to me.

"You know that Noah is losing his mind right now?"

"No, he's not. He's only wishing he had never married me."

"No, he thinks you feel that way. The only reason he didn't follow you is because he knows you feel trapped here, especially since Vlad's father showed up this morning."

"He implied that I wished we never married. I'm pretty certain he's projecting," I said, as my heart felt heavy, and my eyes full of tears. I picked up my wine glass to guzzle more down, only to find a single sip.

This time, I poured myself another glass and topped off Zoe and Faith's. I tried to top off Nora's, but she declined, knowing she had to return to work.

As we paused our conversation to eat, Faith's phone pinged.

"Noah's worried about you. He went home for lunch, and you're not there. Can I tell him you are here?"

I blew out a sigh. "Yeah, I guess."

"I don't have to answer him if you don't want me to."

"No, he shouldn't need to worry about me. I'm not worth it."

"Whoa!" Zoe said, somewhat shocked. "Where did that come from?"

"Let's be real," I said. "I've been more trouble for Noah than I'm worth."

Faith looked up from her phone after she was done texting. "My cousin has never been happier in his life since the two of you got together."

"I doubt that. I mean, he—"

The slamming door interrupted me. Within moments, Noah was on his knees in front of me.

"Babe." His voice was deep and hushed. He put one hand at the base of my neck and lowered my head until our foreheads met. "I heard what you just said. You are worth everything. Every. Last. Damn. Thing. Do you understand me?"

I closed my eyes and shrugged.

"Open your eyes and look at me," he said.

I waited a moment before I followed his directions. As soon as he saw my glazed-over eyes, he began to laugh.

"Aunt Zoe, did you really get my wife drunk in the middle of the afternoon on a weekday?"

"I think she helped," I said. "But this was my doing. Why, you may ask? Because my husband is a pain in my ass!"

Without pause, Noah burst into the loudest, deepest laugh I had ever heard from him. He wrapped me in his arms, and my frustration in him began to melt. I inhaled the sweet wine and vanilla that was him.

"Okay, little brother," Nora said. "This is girls only. Don't you have a job anyway?"

"I could ask the same of you," he replied before returning his attention to me. "I love you, babe. I know I'm an ass, but I'm an ass who loves you and just wants to keep you safe."

He gave me a quick kiss and headed for the door. "I'll see you at home for dinner."

"Noah," I said, and he paused at the threshold. "I love you, too."

He clasped his chest with both hands as though he were reaching for his heart and pretended to melt until he was lying on the floor. After a moment, he bounced to his feet and smiled as he headed back to work.

It was only after he was gone that I said, "Ugh! That man drives me crazy!"

And everyone in the room laughed, including me.

No longer drunk yet relaxed, I wasn't very hungry when dinnertime rolled around, but I managed to eat a few bits of the pasta dish the kitchen at the main house had sent over for us.

When Noah was done eating, he took my hand.

"Do you want to go sit in the den and talk about today?"

I stared at him, saying nothing but thinking about how sexy he was and how I was tired of talking and arguing with him.

"Paige? Do you want to talk?"

"Actually, I think we should go upstairs to our room."

"You want to talk up there? That's fine."

"No, I think I'd rather *not talk* up there."

He tilted his head and smirked.

"Why, Mrs. Foster, are you propositioning me?"

I felt my face turn warm and knew it was flushed from blush.

"Do you want me to be?"

Noah laughed. "Babe, I am a straight man. You are a beautiful woman. Of course I want you to be."

"Well, then, let's go." I let go of his hand and walked ahead of him. "I'll race you to the bed."

We both moved faster as we continued the conversation.

"What's the winner get?" Noah asked, breathing fast as we bounded up the stairs.

"I don't know. You tell me!" I said between giggles.

When we reached the top landing, Noah sped past me and jumped onto the bed. When he did, Paco, who was napping on a pillow, bounced and flew into the air. Noah caught him and Paco swatted angrily at him for disturbing his nap. Noah patted the cat on the head and placed him on the floor.

He was still laughing when I jumped on the bed and landed on top of him.

"You win," I said.

"I most certainly did. I won the day I married you."

Chapter Twenty-Seven

I WAS JARRED AWAKE by the doorbell so rarely used by anyone at Thomas Hall I wasn't sure what it was at first.

Disoriented, I wrapped myself in Noah's fluffy white terrycloth robe as I made my way downstairs. Rain pelted the windows, and the grandfather clock near the front door read nine minutes to ten.

Noah always left a few minutes before nine, and I was usually awake before he left, but he let me sleep that morning. If he kissed me goodbye, I was too tired to notice. The late night in bed had left me happy but exhausted.

When I reached the door, I made my biggest mistake. I didn't ask who was there or check the app Noah downloaded on my phone so I could see the doorbell camera. I swung the front door open and was face-to-face with Alexei and Irena.

They crowded me back from the threshold, and I froze as Alexei closed the door before they made their way into the living room.

"You've gotten lazy living here," Alexei said, looking at the robe.

I managed to move. "We keep different hours here than at Ferma. Why are you here? How did you get onto the estate?"

"It was easy to get in," Alexei began. "Irena got a job at the main house because I paid off the kitchen manager. We met at a bar in town."

"You never told me that," Irena said with her voice full of petulance, but he ignored her.

"Once she began working here, I told her to start fucking the gate guard that works days."

"You've been whoring her out to anyone who suits you." I turned to Irena. "What about Morty? Did your father tell you to fuck him, too, so you could get into the party?"

I rarely said things like this, but the thought went straight through my head and out my mouth.

Alexei slapped me hard. "You've got a lot of nerve using that kind of language after bedding that hui *dick*!"

"He's not a hui! That man is my husband."

He slapped me again, and the sting left me rubbing my face. That was when I knew how much trouble I was in, and adrenaline raced through my veins. Thinking fast was the only way I could escape.

"I'm sorry," I said sheepishly, wanting him to believe he was reverting me back to my Ferma behavior.

Alexei briefly flashed a seemingly unhinged smile, debating on whether to believe my newly formed submission.

"She was good enough that when we drove here in this storm, the guard let me drive her to the house instead of having her walk in the rain. We hid the truck and came here to get you."

"You're coming home with us," Irena exclaimed.

Alexei snapped at her. "Shut up! No one asked for you to speak."

I ignored Alexei's outburst and turned to Irena.

"No, I can't, Irena. I'm married."

She frowned but only for a moment. Then her sinister smirk she inherited from her father formed.

I turned to Alexei and saw the same expression. Panic overflowed from my body.

"What did you do to Noah?" The thought of a world without Noah Foster flashed before my eyes. It was a world I didn't want to live in.

"Nothing yet, child. But one little spark and—"

"BOOM!" Irena squealed in delight.

"Did you really think I was just going to give up on you? You little blyat *whore*. You're coming home now. I own you and your trust fund. You are going to give me babies and money!"

My chest tightened, and I couldn't breathe. Panic was trying to overtake me, but I knew that if Noah and I were going to get through this madness, I had to remain calm. My survival instincts returned effortlessly, like riding a bike.

"I don't really have a choice, then, do I?"

I tried to look defeated, even though I wasn't giving up. I would never return to that hell disguised as a farm. I forced tears until they streamed down my face.

"Skip the tears. I'm not buying that gavno *shit*," Alexei said. Then he reached for my neck and ripped my malachite talisman from my neck before throwing it hard onto the wood floor. I heard it crack when it made impact. "You don't have a choice about the voodoo magic gavno *shit*, either. We'll have none of that in our home."

Alexei grabbed my arm with force and pulled me in the direction of the door.

"I need to change before we go. People will ask questions if they see me in this robe in public."

"Fine," Alexei said, "but give me your damn cellphone. And don't say you don't fucking have one."

Irena's face showed how shocked she was by her father's change in demeanor. However, I had known for over a decade that his piousness was only an act.

I slid the phone from my pocket, shut it off, and handed it to him. It had a difficult password on it, but I wanted to make it as problematic as possible for him if he decided to access it.

"I'll go change. I won't be long."

Alexei grabbed my arm, stopping me in my tracks. His fingertips dug hard into my flesh.

"Don't even think about doing anything stupid, like trying to escape. As a matter of fact, Irena, go with her." He released me with a push.

I lowered my head and raced upstairs with my half-sister following.

When I got to the master suite, I put on my jeans, one of Noah's shirts that was on the floor, and slipped on my Keds. As I did, Irena looked around the room in awe. I couldn't blame her. Our bedrooms at Ferma were tiny with dull beige walls and rough wooden floors containing twin mattresses on the floor and small, simple dressers. Nothing more.

"No wonder you don't want to leave. You have it good here. I thought you might after working at the main house, but I had no idea you had it this good."

I didn't reply but excused myself to use the master bathroom in the hope of buying time. I needed a plan and a way to leave Irena without letting Alexei know.

After brushing my hair and teeth, I opened the bathroom door, exaggerating wiggling the handle.

"Irena, you might want a bathroom break, too. We have a long ride ahead of us."

"That's not a bad idea."

As she closed the door, I said, "Be careful. Sometimes, the lock sticks."

As soon as she closed the door, I locked it from the outside and barricaded it with the chair from the dressing table.

Uncertain what to do, I looked around. I saw the pouch containing my tarot cards on my dresser. I couldn't risk Alexei or Irena destroying them, so I slid the pouch into my back pocket.

Paco hopped onto the bed and stared at me as if he knew something wasn't quite right.

"We are in big trouble, buddy. Any thoughts?"

I barely had the words out of my mouth when Irena said from the other side of the door, "Petya, I think the handle is stuck."

I pretended to try to open it before saying, "Don't panic! I'll go get Father."

Saying the word Father made me want to vomit, but I didn't want to give Irena the sense anything was wrong.

"Okay. Is it okay if I play with your makeup while I wait? I wanted to buy some, but Father said no."

"Go ahead, help yourself."

She was so easily distracted that I knew she'd nearly forget she was trapped in there.

As quietly as possible, I opened the window. Looking down, I wondered if I could make the leap without injuring myself. Paco rubbed against my leg before climbing onto the windowsill. Sensing the danger, he gracefully jumped, landing on his feet. He looked up to me, willing me to join him.

It was only then I noticed the vine-covered trellis on the side of the house and used it to make my way to a safer height before jumping. The landing was hard but, thankfully, not painful. I ran as fast as I could away from the house and down the path that would take me to the production building. I prayed that neither Alexei nor Irena would glance out a window and see me running.

The rain, which had been steady, became heavy. That wave of the storm system brought thunder and lightning, too. As I ran, my frantic thoughts were solely focused on Noah. I had to get to him before it was too late. I couldn't live without him.

While it wasn't even the distance of a football field, the race down the path seemed like the longest of my life. The rain left me soaked long before I reached the building's door. I ran to the empty receptionist's desk, picked up the intercom, and frantically said, "Leave the building immediately. There is a gas leak."

I ran towards Noah's office but collided with him when I turned the corner.

"Paige? What's going on? You are soaking wet. And where did the bruises on your neck come from? Your face is red! Who hit you? I will kill them!"

"Alexei and Irena." My lungs burned, but I continued speaking. He guided me outside as I spoke and others raced out around us. "They came to the house. Tried to make me go with them. Said they were going to blow you up. I escaped through a window and came here."

Faith turned the corner, smiling, unaware of what was going on.

"Paige," she said. "Was that you on the intercom? There's no gas line in this building. It's all electric."

"Oh," I said, confused. "I was told the gas line was cut."

"Let's get everyone back in, out of the rain," Noah said.

Our feet were just over the threshold when a loud crack of thunder rang out, and I flinched. Lightning flashed before striking a metal fence pole next to our house. It must have been enough to ignite the gas line. We watched the gas line near our house ignite, causing a massive explosion. The ground shook, and pieces of the house flew straight into the air, sending wood and bricks flying from a fiery ball and landing in a field of grapevines. The flames from the debris set a few vines alight, and winery workers raced towards them to keep the fire from spreading.

I wrapped my arms tightly around Noah. He embraced me before removing them. "I've got to go help the team."

He took two steps in their direction, stopped, and turned to me, his face ghostly white. I was back in his arms before he said a word.

"Oh, babe. Paco. He was in there. I'm so sorry."

"No, he wasn't. He jumped out the window before I did. I don't know where he went. I hope he's okay."

As if on cue, the orange tabby waltzed over and rubbed against Noah's leg. He picked up the cat and rubbed him behind the ears while breathing a sigh of relief.

"Dude, you scared me."

I stood motionless, watching our house burn. In the distance, I could hear the sirens of the firetrucks heading towards Thomas Hall. The house was demolished. With the exception of my tarot cards, safely tucked in my back pocket, I had lost all of my physical possessions. Again. My thoughts must have shown in my expression because Noah reached out and squeezed my hand after putting Paco inside the winery door.

"It's okay," he whispered in my ear as he stepped behind me and held me tight. "It's just stuff. It can all be replaced. We've got each other and Paco. We'll be fine."

An eternity later, the last of the firefighters and police officers left. Gran had everyone convene at her house to give statements to the authorities. Chief Hayes arrived not long after the firefighters did, and I told him the entire story of Alexei and Irena's arrival that morning.

It didn't take long for the firefighters to find the burned and mangled bodies of Alexei and Irena Orlov. After I identified their remains, the funeral home arranged to ship their cremated remains back to Ferma. I sent them to Yuri with a note, explaining what happened to all three of them. Though I did not know what Alexei had done with Vlad's body, I was doing the right thing. While I prayed Alexei's death would be the end of the cult, deep in my gut, I knew it would continue. However, I was finally free of the Orlov cult, once and for all.

I was exhausted and had battled a headache from the smoke and adrenaline by the time Noah and I went to bed in the Elizabeth room. It was one of the many guest suites at the main house. When we first went into it, Gran had arranged for pajamas and robes for us, as well as a set of clothes for the next day.

After a long shower, we sat in bed. Noah was drinking coffee while I enjoyed a cup of ginger peach tea. My eyes were closed when Noah's warm breath brushed against my ear.

"Babe, are you okay?" he whispered.

"Yeah, just overwhelmed. Today has been—well, it's been a lot."

"It has. Don't worry, though. I talked to Gran while you were giving your statement to the police. We are going to move into the pool house while our place is being rebuilt."

I nodded, and he squeezed me tight.

"I think I just need to sleep for a while," I said, and he took my teacup from me and placed it on the nightstand. After, he turned off the lights and spooned against me. I was dozing off when Noah said, "If you wake in the morning, and I'm not here, I'm going to a security meeting."

I was safe, but Noah would spend the rest of his life guaranteeing no one would ever try to take me away from Thomas Hall.

Epilogue

One Year Later

I T WAS MEMORIAL DAY, and the start of summer arrived hotter and more humid than usual. When I pulled back the curtains of our bedroom, it revealed a beautiful morning. We moved into our new home a few days earlier, and much of the house was still in boxes.

Gran had hoped to get everything in order while we were away on a belated honeymoon celebrating our first wedding anniversary. However, the house wasn't finished, making her plan impossible to execute.

We could see the pool from the window and staff members were setting up tables and coolers for Cassandra's annual Memorial Day pool party. It was mostly family, but I had been extended an invitation for three years before we married when I worked at the brewery. It was always fun, and I loved that I got to spend the day near Noah. Back then, it was a rare treat.

As I watched, Noah walked up behind me and wrapped his arms around my waist. I leaned into him and let out a content sigh.

He nibbled on my ear before whispering, "How's my wife this morning?"

"Good. I'm looking forward to the pool party. And time with you. We've both been so busy lately."

"I know I've been spending more time than usual attending to the vines, and you have been working hard at Tea & Tarot," Noah said as he left a trail of kisses down my neck and across my collarbone until he reached the edge of my robe.

As he did, Paco wove himself between our ankles.

"Who knew it would be so popular? I was happy my trust fund was more than enough to cover the startup expenses, but I never expected it to turn a profit in less than a year."

"Your trust fund covered much more than that. You're wealthier than I am now."

"Yeah, but I don't need it. Aside from buying the new car, I already owned everything I wanted and needed."

"Having Tea & Tarot has really made you happy, hasn't it?"

"It has and not just me. Gran loves to play hostess. I worry she's pushing herself too hard, but she swears she's not. I think she just likes having her cards read when we are done."

"What does she ask about?" he asked.

"If there are there more great grandbabies in her future? I think it's a not-so-subtle hint."

"Speaking of, have you heard?"

"That Hope's pregnant again? Yes. Faith told me. She also told me that Ben is pushing for a baby. She wants to wait."

"Well, they just got married, and Faith is young. They have plenty of time."

"It's hard to believe they got married a month ago," I said. "There must have been close to three hundred people there. I know she wanted a small wedding, but Ben and her mom convinced her to use the church and the country club."

"You looked spectacular as her bridesmaid." As he spoke, he slid my robe off my body and turned me to face him. "But I like you better this way."

I smirked and shook my head. After one of his head-spinning kisses, he whispered in my ear, "The party isn't for a few hours. Wanna work on making that baby we keep talking about?"

"With you, always."

THE END

Acknowledgements

This novel is a testament to the fact that I watch too many documentaries about escaping cults. So many, in fact, that it inspired a character I first introduced in the novella, *If I Can Do This Again.* However, not even I could have imagined Paige WIlson would end up with her own full-length story.

I knew early on that I wanted Paige to be a tarot card reading, amulet wearing, cat owner. Not being proficient in any of these things, research and assistance was vital.

First, I turned to Zachary Longtine and Emily Albo for help with the tarot cards. Their guidance, along with several books on the subject, gave me the confidence to piece together the type of readings that Paige would have formulated.

In addition to being the best book therapist ever, when it comes to amulets, gems, and stones, Stefanie Lewis is my go to person. She was kind enough to spend multiple nights with me researching the stones that best met my main characters needs and the best way to weave them into the story.

As for the subject of cats, I went to the source. Paco Brown, my neighbor's cat, provided excellent guidance on how to write about cats. And for the record, yes, this is the cat that inspired Paige's Paco, right down to being orange.

Of course, research alone doesn't get a book to the finish line. A team of beta readers you can trust is essential. Jen Laning, Stefanie Lewis, Kathy Hawkins, and Dezi Webler are phenomenal women who take the time out of their busy lives to help me bring my vision to life. For this novel, I advised them of the dark themes in advance. However, even the one who passed on this project for personal reasons, took the time to talk with me about trigger warnings and respectful approaches when writing. Sometimes being a great beta reader doesn't necessarily mean reading.

Writing never ends with a completed draft. The right editor and a great proofreader make the difference in the final product. Samantha Pico at The Goth Editor, formerly Miss Eloquent Edits, is both the editor and proofreader who polishes my idea and gets it ready for release. And she always does it wonderfully.

We are told never to judge a book by its cover. However, without the right cover, a book may never draw enough attention to get picked up by a reader. The cover for *Protecting Paige*, and the other books in *The Baker Family Legacy Series*, were put together by GetCovers.com. They bring my vision to life in ways I never could imagine.

About The Author

B ETH SORENSEN IS A Virginia native who graduated from Old Dominion University with an undergraduate degree in Geography. She is a cancer survivor currently living in rural North Carolina with her husband and enjoys good wine, great food, and a quiet beach.

Check out her website at http://bethsoren.com to learn more about Beth and her novels.

Also by Beth Sorensen

<u>The Thomas Hall Series</u>

Crush at Thomas Hall

Divorcing a Dead Man

Waiting for Time to Tell

If I Can Do This Again: A Thomas Hall Novella

Things She Can Never Know: A Thomas Hall Novella

<u>The Baker Legacy Series</u>

Handling Hope

Finding Faith

Protecting Paige

Welcome to The Oyster Bar: a story of love & death